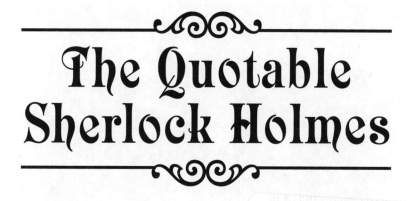

The Quotable Sherlock Holmes

The Quotable Sherlock Holmes

BY JOHN H. WATSON, M.D.

WITH AN INTRODUCTION BY JOHN H. WATSON III
ASSISTED BY GERARD VAN DER LEUN

THE MYSTERIOUS PRESS
Published by Warner Books

A Time Warner Company

Copyright ©2000 by Gerard Van der Leun
All rights reserved.

Mysterious Press Books are published by Warner Books, Inc.,
1271 Avenue of the Americas, New York, NY 10020

Visit our Web site at www.twbookmark.com

A Time Warner Company
The Mysterious Press name and logo are trademarks of Warner Books

Printed in the United States of America
First Printing: November 2000
10 9 8 7 6 5 4 3 2 1

Library of Congress Cataloging-in-Publication Data
Doyle, Arthur Conan, Sir, 1859-1930.
    The quotable Sherlock Holmes / [selected] by Gerard van der Leun.
      p. cm.
    ISBN 0-446-67727-2
    1. Holmes, Sherlock (Fictitious character)—Quotations, maxims, etc. 2. Doyle, Arthur Conan, Sir, 1859-1930—Quotations. 3. Murder—Investigation—Quotations, maxims, etc. 4. Private investigators—Quotations, maxims, etc. 5. Quotations, English. I. Van der Leun, Gerard, 1945- II. Title.

PR4621 .V36 2000
828'.802--dc21
                                                                    00-040108

Book design and text composition by Ellen Gleeson
Cover design by Rachel McClain
Cover illustration by Sidney Paget
Interior illustrations by Sidney Paget

"My name is Sherlock Holmes. It is my business to know what other people don't know."

—*The Adventure of the Blue Carbuncle*

❦ Contents ❧

∾ A Brief Introductory Note ∾
ON DR. JOHN H. WATSON'S NEWLY
DISCOVERED MANUSCRIPT

By His Great-Grandson John H. Watson III

While it is indubitably the case that my great-grandfather's fame rests on the chronicles of his famous partner in crime, Mr. Sherlock Holmes, it is often overlooked that the fame of the world's first "consulting detective" would simply not exist without Dr. John H. Watson. Never one to popularize his cases, Holmes, without my grandfather's steady hand, head, and sense of history, would simply have allowed his trove of notes and scattered case files to be shipped off to some stash of scholars' trivia in the sub-subbasement of an obscure university library, there to languish until some student, desperate for a thesis, dug it out to provide the world with one of those carefully constructed and terminally enervating tomes that pass for "an original contribution to knowledge" in these blighted times.

Indeed, the odds were heavily stacked in favor of obscurity for Holmes had not my great-grandfather chanced upon him in London after his return from service to his Queen and Country in

Afghanistan. As a result, both myself and my father, John H. Watson II, have always held among ourselves that the world is the richer not for one or the other of these exceptional individuals, but for what they made in combination. Because of this the Watson family, such as it was and such as it has become, has always remained alert for every opportunity to remind passionate Holmsians around the world of our family motto: "Without Watson, no Holmes." Or, as Holmes himself so pithily put it, "Where would I be without my Boswell?" Where indeed?

Accordingly, when I came into possession of the sheaf of papers that form the body of this small but essential addition to the Holmes Canon my duty was clear, and no scion of the Watson clan has ever shirked duty when it called.

I confess at this juncture to being, at first, baffled by my discovery. I had been living a secluded life quite removed from the cares and bustle of the modern world in my chosen retreat just outside of a small town in a western Canadian province (which modesty and a need for solitude even now compel me to conceal), when a letter from my family's solicitors in London roused me from my pastoral stupor.

It seemed that a team of immigrant workmen (fortunately overseen by a foreman of solid Cornish stock) had, while renovating what once had been my great-grandfather's London digs, uncovered a small closet at the back of my great-grandfather's surgery. It had been sealed and covered with wallpaper at some time in the 1930s. The building had since changed hands and gone through several incarnations, from Blitz target to rooming house to gentrified flats. Within that closet, amongst the dust and detritus that bore mute testimony to the decades it had been undisturbed, was a sealed tea chest with a label in my great-grandfather's hand designating it as the property of one "John H. Watson, M.D."

After some inquiries, the Cornish foreman delivered it to my family's solicitors. Trusty men that they are, the solicitors—upon determining my status as the sole surviving heir to the Watson estate—informed me of the existence of the chest and the fact that they were shipping it to me forthwith in an unopened state. I was, of course, suitably intrigued by this, but saddened by the fact that, trustworthy as they might be, the solicitors were also quite penurious and had shipped the chest via sea and land rather than using the somewhat more expensive but expedient method of air freight. As a result I had to temper my expectations and possess myself in patience for the four months it took the chest to arrive.

During this time my meditations on this unexpected harbinger from the past were fraught with fantasy. What if the chest contained tales of my great-grandfather and his famous companion? That would be an unexpected bonanza that all the world would relish and enjoy. Surely, to expand "The Watson-Holmes Canon" with fresh material—no matter how unfinished—would bring delight to untold millions throughout the world, as well as help me continue my own research into the breeding of a curly-haired Corgi which I had one day hoped to present to the Queen. Indeed, many dreams would be solved by such a coup. Mine not the least of them.

But dreams are sometimes made to be broken, and, to some degree, this proved true of my own. Upon arrival, I set the chest on my desk and merely gazed at it for several cups of tea. Finally I gathered up my hopes and courage and, with the aid of a trusty if rusted crowbar, pried off the top of the chest.

It seemed as if the very odor of those long-ago gaslit evenings of London winters of sleet and a thick pea-soup fog embraced my small room. Gazing down into the shredded excelsior that formed the packing, I descried a small leather bag. I removed it carefully, for it was brittle with age, and carried it to the linoleum table in my kitchen, where I could bring a bright light to bear upon it. Affixed to the outside was a small if tarnished silver plaque with the inscription "To Watson. In appreciation, S. Holmes." You may well imagine my excitement upon seeing this fresh evidence of the legendary association. Indeed, I felt my pulse rate climb to unhealthy heights for a brief period.

Tripping the catch I opened the bag and, I must confess, was immediately and utterly disappointed. Instead of folded manuscripts gushing from the cracked leather opening, I descried only the faint glint of antique medical instruments and a number of bottles and flasks from which the contents had long since evaporated or decayed. It was only upon a second, closer inspection that I noticed a sheaf of foolscap, bound in the red ribbon common for legal complaints, lying at the bottom of the bag under a jumble of bottles and instruments.

I removed the tied bundle and carefully cut the ribbon to unfold it and let it see the light for the first time in nearly a hundred years.

It took only a sliver of an instant for me to recognize the precise copperplate hand of my great-grandfather on the top sheet, which said "Holmes—Sayings Worth Noting." And on the following sheets a carefully compiled and corrected collection of those things Sherlock Holmes had said that my great-grandfather had found, upon reflection, worth saving in one place. From the faint shakiness of his otherwise stalwart script and the completeness of the material, I can only assume that—while undated—the manuscript had been written out by him in the deep autumn of his years, long after his boon companion had gone to his reward, and Watson was left alone with only the fading coals of his memory to warm him.

Now, it was evident that all in this manuscript had been said before and that my great-grandfather was merely taking, if you will, a victory lap through his work before the fall of night; but it was and remains a genuine John H. Watson manuscript, and, as a Watson—the last of that name and the line—my duty to see it to publication was clear. But how?

Having been a recluse for many years here in the Canadian outback with only my Corgis to sustain and comfort me, I was unfamiliar with the labyrinthine ways of modern publishing and ignorant of how to obtain a relationship with a firm that would bring these last notes of my illustrious ancestor to an admiring public. Indeed, the task daunted me for many months until, one dark and stormy night, I lay awake perusing the latest issue of the monthly newsletter *The Corgi Companion* and noted an exceptionally concise and pithy article on the difficulties of getting a new publisher for the essential *Corgi Bloodlines*—a volume of Corgi genealogy that is the bible of breeders such as myself. The author of this article related, in riveting detail, his search for a publisher that would undertake this mammoth project in the face of an indifferent world. That he had, through determination and sheer grit, succeeded in this seemingly impossible quest awoke in me only blind admiration. Suffice it to say that the post took my tale and my quandary to him the very next day.

As fate would have it, Mr. Gerard Van der Leun was not only a devoted Corgi breeder such as myself but highly conversant with the work of my late great-grandfather. After an extended exchange of letters on the subjects at hand, he elected to become my champion and to put his shoulder to the wheel. And while the task may have been Sisyphean if not Stygian at times, you see its fruits before you.

It is the firm opinion of Mr. Van der Leun and myself that, while the proceeds from this publication will not be of copious sums as to permit us to complete our respective Corgi breeding projects (thus lightening and brightening our Queen's declining years with a shedless but cozy Corgi), it still merits some small attention from the world. Indeed, with the publication of this work, possibly the last ever penned by my great-grandfather, it is our fond hope that the efforts of all involved may bring to you, dear reader, an opportunity to once more refresh yourself by drinking deep of the words of the individual my own great-grandfather once called "the best and the wisest man whom I have ever known."

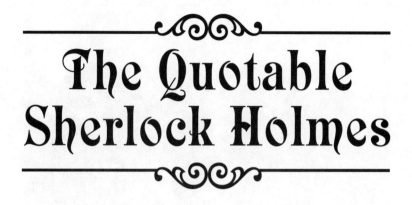

The Quotable
Sherlock Holmes

"The Only Unofficial Consulting Detective"

SHERLOCK HOLMES: HIS LIMITS

1. Knowledge of Literature: Nil.
2. Knowledge of Philosophy: Nil.
3. Knowledge of Astronomy: Nil.
4. Knowledge of Politics: Feeble.
5. Knowledge of Botany: Variable. Well up in belladonna, opium, and poisons generally. Knows nothing of practical gardening.
6. Knowledge of Geology: Practical but limited. Tells at a glance different soils from each other. After walks has shown me splashes upon his trousers, and told me by their color and consistence in what part of London he had received them.
7. Knowledge of Chemistry: Profound.
8. Knowledge of Anatomy: Accurate but unsystematic.
9. Knowledge of Sensational Literature: Immense. He appears to know every detail of every horror perpetrated in the century.

10. Plays the violin well.
11. Is an expert singlestick player, boxer, and swordsman.
12. Has a good practical knowledge of British law.

—A Study in Scarlet

FAMILY

"My ancestors were country squires, who appear to have led much the same life as is natural to their class. But, none the less, my turn that way is in my veins, and may have come with my grandmother, who was the sister of Vernet, the French artist."

—The Greek Interpreter

THE COURT OF LAST RESORT

"The only unofficial consulting detective. I am the last and highest court of appeal in detection."

—The Sign of Four

AGE

"I trust that age doth not wither nor custom stale my infinite variety."

—The Adventure of the Empty House

His Profession

"Well, I have a trade of my own. I suppose I am the only one in the world. I'm a consulting detective, if you can understand what that is. Here in London we have lots of government detectives and lots of private ones. When these fellows are at fault, they come to me, and I manage to put them on the right scent. They lay all the evidence before me, and I am generally able, by the help of my knowledge of the history of crime, to set them straight. There is a strong family resemblance about misdeeds, and if you have all the details of a thousand at your finger ends, it is odd if you can't unravel the thousand and first."

—A Study in Scarlet

Basic Skills

"My eyes have been trained to examine faces and not their trimmings. It is the first quality of a criminal investigator that he should see through a disguise."

—The Hound of the Baskervilles

His Brief Career in British Intelligence

"Things were going wrong, and no one could understand why they were going wrong. Agents were suspected or even caught, but there was evidence of some strong and secret central force. It was absolutely necessary to expose it. Strong pressure was brought upon me to look into the matter. It has cost me two years, Watson, but they have not been devoid of excitement. When I say that I started my pilgrimage at Chicago, graduated in an Irish secret society at Buffalo, gave serious trouble to the constabulary at Skibbareen, and so eventually caught the eye of a subordinate agent of Von Bork, who recommended me as a likely man, you will realize that the matter was complex. Since then I have been honored by his confidence, which has not prevented most of his plans going subtly wrong and five of his best agents being in prison."

—His Last Bow

His Calming Effect on Crime

"Besides, on general principles it is best that I should not leave the country. Scotland Yard feels lonely without me, and it causes an unhealthy excitement among the criminal classes."

—The Disappearance of Lady Frances Carfax

His Chosen Aerobic Routine

"If you could have looked into Allardyce's back shop, you would have seen a dead pig swung from a hook in the ceiling, and a gentleman in his shirt sleeves furiously stabbing at it with this spear. I was that energetic person, and I have satisfied myself that by no exertion of my strength can I transfix the pig with a single blow."

—The Adventure of Black Peter

His College Chum

"You never heard me talk of Victor Trevor? He was the only friend I made during the two years I was at college. I was never a very sociable fellow, always rather fond of moping in my rooms and working out my own little methods of thought, so that I never mixed much with the men of my year. Bar fencing and boxing I had few athletic tastes, and then my line of study was quite distinct from that of the other fellows, so that we had no points of contact at all. Trevor was the only man I knew, and that only through the accident of his bull terrier freezing on to my ankle one morning as I went down to chapel."

—The "Gloria Scott"

His Enduring Motivation

"I play the game for the game's own sake."

—The Adventure of the Bruce-Partington Plans

HIS NET WORTH

"Between ourselves, the recent cases in which I have been of assistance to the royal family of Scandinavia, and to the French republic, have left me in such a position that I could continue to live in the quiet fashion which is most congenial to me, and to concentrate my attention upon my chemical researches."

—*The Final Problem*

CAN HE GET A WITNESS?

"Do not dream of going, Watson, for I very much prefer having a witness, if only as a check to my own memory."

—*The Adventure of the Noble Bachelor*

CURRENT CASES ON HAND

"Some ten or twelve, but none which present any feature of interest. They are important, you understand, without being interesting."

—*A Case of Identity*

DON'T MENTION IT

"I should prefer that you do not mention my name at all in connection with the case, as I choose to be only associated with those crimes which present some difficulty in their solution."

—*The Adventure of the Cardboard Box*

Drama, Love of

"Watson here will tell you that I never can resist a touch of the dramatic."

—*The Naval Treaty*

Work, Work, Work

"My mind rebels at stagnation. Give me problems, give me work, give me the most abstruse cryptogram, or the most intricate analysis, and I am in my own proper atmosphere. I can dispense then with artificial stimulants."

—*The Sign of Four*

He Goes on the Lam

"I have my plans laid, and all will be well. Matters have gone so far now that they can move without my help as far as the arrest goes, though my presence is necessary for a conviction. It is obvious, therefore, that I cannot do better than get away for the few days which remain before the police are at liberty to act. It would be a great pleasure to me, therefore, if you could come on to the Continent with me."

—The Final Problem

Just Mention My Name

"They have the crown down at Hurlstone—though they had some legal bother and a considerable sum to pay before they were allowed to retain it. I am sure that if you mentioned my name they would be happy to show it to you."

—The Musgrave Ritual

The Limits of the Mind

"There are limits, you see, to our friend's intelligence. It would have been a coup-mattre had he deduced what I would deduce and acted accordingly."

—The Final Problem

MORE ABOUT HIS LIMITATIONS

"I fear that if the matter is beyond humanity it is certainly beyond me."

—The Adventure of the Devil's Foot

LONDON'S LUCK

"It is fortunate for this community that I am not a criminal."

—The Adventure of the Bruce-Partington Plans

NOT A LOVER

"I have never loved, Watson, but if I did and if the woman I loved had met such an end, I might have done as our lawless lion-hunter has done."

—The Adventure of the Devil's Foot

ON BEING HELD IN RESERVE

"I remain an unknown factor in the business, ready to throw in all my weight at a critical moment."

—The Hound of the Baskervilles

One Punch

"It was a straight left against a slogging ruffian. I emerged as you see me. Mr. Woodley went home in a cart."

—*The Adventure of the Solitary Cyclist*

Perils of a High-Performance Mind

"My mind is like a racing engine, tearing itself to pieces because it is not connected up with the work for which it was built."

—*The Adventure of Wisteria Lodge*

Signs of Manic-Depression

"Let me see—what are my other shortcomings? I get in the dumps at times, and don't open my mouth for days on end. You must not think I am sulky when I do that. Just let me alone, and I'll soon be right. What have you to confess now? It's just as well for two fellows to know the worst of one another before they begin to live together."

—*A Study in Scarlet*

Summing Up

"I think that I may go as far as to say that I have not lived wholly in vain. If my record were closed tonight I could still survey it with equanimity. The air of London is the sweeter for my presence. In over a thousand cases I am not aware that I have ever used my powers upon the wrong side. Of late I have been tempted to look into the problems furnished by nature rather than those more superficial ones for which our artificial state of society is responsible."

—*The Final Problem*

His Last Will and Testament

"I write these few lines through the courtesy of Mr. Moriarty, who awaits my convenience for the final discussion of those questions which lie between us. He has been giving me a sketch of the methods by which he avoided the English police and kept himself informed of our movements. They certainly confirm the very high opinion which I had formed of his abilities. I am pleased to think that I shall be able to free society from any further effects of his presence, though I fear that it is at a cost which will give pain to my friends, and especially, my dear Watson, to you. I have already explained to you, however, that my career had in any case reached its crisis, and that no possible conclusion to it could be more congenial to me than this. Indeed, if I may make a full confession to you, I was quite convinced that the letter from Meiringen was a hoax, and I allowed you to depart on that errand under the persuasion that some development of this sort would follow. Tell Inspector Patterson that the papers which he needs to convict the gang are in pigeonhole M., done up in a blue envelope and inscribed 'Moriarty.' I made every disposition of my property before leaving England and handed it to my brother Mycroft. Pray give my greetings to Mrs. Watson, and believe me to be, my dear fellow,

"Very sincerely yours,
"SHERLOCK HOLMES."

—The Final Problem

His Defeats
"I have been beaten four times—three times by men, and once by a woman."

—The Five Orange Pips

His Raison d'Etre
"Because it is my desire. Is that not enough?"

—The Adventure of the Dying Detective

His Own Worst Enemy

"I suspect myself. Of coming to conclusions too rapidly."

—*The Naval Treaty*

His Reading List

"I read nothing except the criminal news and the agony column. The latter is always instructive."

—*The Adventure of the Noble Bachelor*

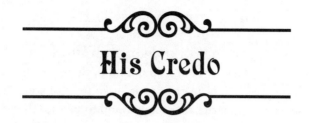

His Credo

Brainwork and the Meaning of Life

"I cannot live without brainwork. What else is there to live for? Stand at the window here. Was ever such a dreary, dismal, unprofitable world? See how the yellow fog swirls down the street and drifts across the duncoloured houses. What could be more hopelessly prosaic and material? What is the use of having powers, Doctor, when one has no field upon which to exert them? Crime is commonplace, existence is commonplace, and no qualities save those which are commonplace have any function upon earth."

—The Sign of Four

Law, Staying on the Right Side of

"In over a thousand cases I am not aware that I have ever used my powers upon the wrong side."

—The Final Problem

FACTS, WHEN NOT TO GET IN FRONT OF THEM

"I have not all my facts yet but I do not think there are any insuperable difficulties. Still, it is an error to argue in front of your data. You find yourself insensibly twisting them round to fit your theories."

—*The Adventure of Wisteria Lodge*

WILL WORK FOR EXPENSES

"As to reward, my profession is its own reward; but you are at liberty to defray whatever expenses I may be put to, at the time which suits you best."

—*The Adventure of the Speckled Band*

THE RIGHT ATMOSPHERE

"It is a singular thing, but I find that a concentrated atmosphere helps a concentration of thought. I have not pushed it to the length of getting into a box to think, but that is the logical outcome of my convictions. Have you turned the case over in your mind?"

—*The Hound of the Baskervilles*

Will Work for Stimulation

"Even the most insignificant problem would be welcome in these stagnant days."

—*The Adventure of the Missing Three-Quarter*

Wings on Criminals Highly Unlikely at This Time

"I have investigated many crimes, but I have never yet seen one which was committed by a flying creature. As long as the criminal remains upon two legs so long must there be some indentation, some abrasion, some trifling displacement which can be detected by the scientific searcher."

—*The Adventure of Black Peter*

Work Is Its Own Reward

"I examine the data, as an expert, and pronounce a specialist's opinion. I claim no credit in such cases. My name figures in no newspaper. The work itself, the pleasure of finding a field for my peculiar powers, is my highest reward."

—*The Sign of Four*

How to Furnish Your Brain

"I consider that a man's brain originally is like a little empty attic, and you have to stock it with such furniture as you choose. A fool takes in all the lumber of every sort that he comes across, so that the knowledge which might be useful to him gets crowded out, or at best is jumbled up with a lot of other things, so that he has a difficulty in laying his hands upon it. Now the skillful workman is very careful indeed as to what he takes into his brain-attic. He will have nothing but the tools which may help him in doing his work, but of these he has a large assortment, and all in the most perfect order. It is a mistake to think that that room has elastic walls and can distend to any extent. Depend upon it there comes a time when for every addition of knowledge you forget something that you knew before. It is of the highest importance, therefore, not to have useless facts elbowing out the useful ones."

—*A Study in Scarlet*

"I Have Some Knowledge, However, of Baritsu": Arts, Martial and Otherwise

MARTIAL ARTS

"I have some knowledge, however, of baritsu, or the Japanese system of wrestling, which has more than once been very useful to me."

—*The Adventure of the Empty House*

GERMAN

"Though unmusical, German is the most expressive of all languages."

—*His Last Bow*

AMERICAN LINGO

"American slang is very expressive sometimes."

—*The Adventure of the Noble Bachelor*

ON NARRATIVE DRIVE

"Tell us what you can, but stop when you are tired and keep up your strength with a little stimulant."

—The Adventure of the Engineer's Thumb

ART, FORMS OF

"Art in the blood is liable to take the strangest forms."

—The Greek Interpreter

COOKS, LIMITATIONS OF

"Her cuisine is limited but she has as good an idea of breakfast as a Scotchwoman."

—The Naval Treaty

GERMAN MUSIC

"I observe that there is a good deal of German music on the program, which is more to my taste than Italian or French. It is introspective and I want to introspect."

—The Red-Headed League

GOETHE

"Goethe is always pithy."

—The Sign of Four

THE LIMITS OF CONCISION

"I will compress the story as far as may be done without omitting anything vital to the case."

—*The Crooked Man*

MACHIAVELLI AND PURE REASON

"Perhaps there are points which have escaped your Machiavellian intellect. Let us consider the problem in the light of pure reason. This man's reference is to a book. That is our point of departure."

—*The Valley of Fear*

PLEASURES OF ART

"To the man who loves art for its own sake it is frequently in its least important and lowliest manifestations that the keenest pleasure is to be derived."

—*The Adventure of the Copper Beeches*

ON PLOT

"The plot thickens."

—*A Study in Scarlet*

❦

Detection,
the Lifestyle

THE EXACT SCIENCE

"Detection is, or ought to be, an exact science and should be treated in the same cold and unemotional manner. You have attempted to tinge it with romanticism, which produces much the same effect as if you worked a love-story or an elopement into the fifth proposition of Euclid."

—*The Sign of Four*

THE CONNOISSEUR OF CRIME

"Breadth of view is one of the essentials of our profession. The interplay of ideas and the oblique uses of knowledge are often of extraordinary interest. You will excuse these remarks from one who, though a mere connoisseur of crime, is still rather older and perhaps more experienced than yourself."

—*The Valley of Fear*

On Circularity, in Crime and Life

"Mr. Mac, the most practical thing that you ever did in your life would be to shut yourself up for three months and read twelve hours a day at the annals of crime. Everything comes in circles. . . .The old wheel turns, and the same spoke comes up. It's all been done before, and will be again."

—The Valley of Fear

Death Threats

"The old sweet song. How often have I heard it in days gone by. It was a favorite ditty of the late lamented Professor Moriarty. Colonel Sebastian Moran has also been known to warble it. And yet I live and keep bees upon the South Downs."

—His Last Bow

Challenge of Crime

"There are no crimes and no criminals in these days. What is the use of having brains in our profession? I know well that I have it in me to make my name famous. No man lives or has ever lived who has brought the same amount of study and of natural talent to the detection of crime which I have done. And what is the result? There is no crime to detect, or, at most, some bungling villainy with a motive so transparent that even a Scotland Yard official can see through it."

—*A Study in Scarlet*

THE DRAMA OF A DETECTIVE'S LIFE

"Watson insists that I am the dramatist in real life. Some touch of the artist wells up within me, and calls insistently for a well-staged performance."

—*The Valley of Fear*

ADVERSITY, THE THRILL OF

"There is nothing more stimulating than a case where everything goes against you."

—*The Hound of the Baskervilles*

CHATEAU ETHER

"A remarkable wine. Our friend upon the sofa has assured me that it is from Franz Josef's special cellar at the Schoenbrunn Palace. Might I trouble you to open the window, for chloroform vapor does not help the palate."

—*His Last Bow*

THE BEGINNING, END OF

"Our difficulties are not over. Our police work ends, but our legal work begins."

—*The Adventure of Wisteria Lodge*

GOES WITH THE TERRITORY

"Danger is part of my trade."

—*The Final Problem*

HEAVENLY CARES

"What the deuce is the solar system to me? You say that we go round the sun. If we went round the moon it would not make a pennyworth of difference to me or to my work."

—*A Study in Scarlet*

RENTING BAKER STREET

"I have my eye on a suite in Baker Street which would suit us down to the ground. You don't mind the smell of strong tobacco, I hope?"

—*A Study in Scarlet*

THE HUMAN TARGET

"This man's occupation is gone. He is lost if he returns to London. If I read his character right he will devote his whole energies to revenging himself upon me. He said as much in our short interview, and I fancy that he meant it. I should certainly recommend you to return to your practice."

—The Final Problem

JUST ONE OF THOSE DAYS

"Professor Moriarty is not a man who lets the grass grow under his feet. I went out about midday to transact some business in Oxford Street. As I passed the corner which leads from Bentinck Street on to the Welbeck Street crossing a two-horse van furiously driven whizzed round and was on me like a flash. I sprang for the foot-path and saved myself by the fraction of a second. The van dashed round by Marylebone Lane and was gone in an instant. I kept to the pavement after that, but as I walked down Vere Street a brick came down from the roof of one of the houses and was shattered to fragments at my feet. I called the police and had the place examined. There were slates and bricks piled up on the roof preparatory to some repairs, and they would have me believe that the wind had toppled over one of these. Of course I knew better, but I could prove nothing. I took a cab after that and reached my brother's rooms in Pall Mall, where I spent the day. Now I have come round to you, and on my way I was attacked by a rough with a bludgeon. I knocked him down, and the police have him in custody; but I can tell you with the most absolute confidence that no possible connection will ever be traced between the gentleman upon whose front teeth I have barked my knuckles and the retiring mathematical coach, who is, I daresay, working out problems upon a black-board ten miles away. You will not wonder that my first act on entering your rooms was to close your shutters, and that I have been compelled to ask your permission to leave the house by some less conspicuous exit than the front door."

—*The Final Problem*

His Modest Achievements

"In a modest way I have combated evil, but to take on the Father of Evil himself would, perhaps, be too ambitious a task."

—*The Hound of the Baskervilles*

Living, His

"I have taken to living by my wits."

—*The Musgrave Ritual*

The Curse of the Detective's Mind

"It is one of the curses of a mind with a turn like mine that I must look at everything with reference to my own special subject. You look at these scattered houses, and you are impressed by their beauty. I look at them, and the only thought which comes to me is a feeling of their isolation and of the impunity with which crime may be committed there."

—The Adventure of the Copper Beeches

Genius

"They say that genius is an infinite capacity for taking pains. It's a very bad definition, but it does apply to detective work."

—A Study in Scarlet

He Begins to See the Light

"The clouds lighten, though I should not venture to say that the danger is over."

—The Man with the Twisted Lip

Elementary

CLEARING UP, HOW TO
"Nothing clears up a case so much as stating it to another person."

—Silver Blaze

DOG, THE FAMOUS DO-NOTHING
"Is there any point to which you would wish to draw my attention?"

"To the curious incident of the dog in the night-time."

"The dog did nothing in the night-time."

"That was the curious incident."

—Silver Blaze

CHASMS, GETTING OUT OF THEM
"Well, then, about that chasm. I had no serious difficulty in getting out of it, for the very simple reason that I never was in it."

—The Adventure of the Empty House

THE COMPELLING NEED
"Data! Data! Data! I can make no bricks without clay!"
—*The Adventure of the Copper Beeches*

ENDINGS
"Come, friend Watson, the curtain rings up for the last act."
—*The Adventure of the Second Stain*

THE VALUE OF UNIMPORTANT MATTERS
"Indeed, I have found that it is usually in unimportant matters that there is a field for the observation, and for the quick analysis of cause and effect which gives the charm to an investigation."
—*A Case of Identity*

FORCEFUL FACTS
"Each fact is suggestive in itself. Together they have a cumulative force."
—*The Adventure of the Bruce-Partington Plans*

Getting a Grip

"Let us get a firm grip of the very little which we do know, so that when fresh facts arise we may be ready to fit them into their places."

—*The Adventure of the Devil's Foot*

Give Only the Essentials, Please

"Some facts should be suppressed, or, at least, a just sense of proportion should be observed in treating them. The only point in the case which deserved mention was the curious analytical reasoning from effects to causes, by which I succeeded in unraveling it."

—*The Sign of Four*

Let Caution Be Your Guide

"Bear in mind one of the phrases in that queer old legend and avoid the moor in those hours of darkness when the powers of evil are exalted."

—*The Hound of the Baskervilles*

The Nature of Circumstance

"Circumstantial evidence is a very tricky thing. It may seem to point very straight to one thing, but if you shift your own point of view a little, you may find it pointing in an equally uncompromising manner to something entirely different."

—*The Boscombe Valley Mystery*

THE NATURE OF GUESSING

"It is the scientific use of the imagination, but we always have some material basis on which to start our speculation."

—*The Hound of the Baskervilles*

SMALL POINT

"Elementary. It is one of those instances where the reasoner can produce an effect which seems remarkable to his neighbor, because the latter has missed the one little point which is the basis of the deduction."

—*The Crooked Man*

Etiquette

ADVERSE FIRST IMPRESSIONS

"I do not know whether it came from his own innate depravity or from the promptings of his master, but he was rude enough to set a dog at me. Neither dog nor man liked the look of my stick, however, and the matter fell through. Relations were strained after that, and further inquiries out of the question."

—*The Adventure of the Missing Three-Quarter*

DINING OUT ON STORIES

"Experience may be of value, you know; you have only to put it into words to gain the reputation of being excellent company for the remainder of your existence."

—*The Adventure of the Engineer's Thumb*

DISCRETION

"One has to be discreet when one talks of high matters of state."

—*The Adventure of the Bruce-Partington Plans*

DISTANCE, KEEPING ONE'S
"If you approach me, Watson, I shall order you out of the house."
—*The Adventure of the Dying Detective*

THE DOOR, CLOSING IT
"Your conversation is most entertaining. When you go out close the door, for there is a decided draught."
—*The Adventure of the Speckled Band*

DUTY
"It's every man's business to see justice done."
—*The Crooked Man*

INVITATIONS
"My correspondence has certainly the charm of variety, and the humbler are usually the more interesting. This looks like one of those unwelcome social summonses which call upon a man either to be bored or to lie."
—*The Adventure of the Noble Bachelor*

Social Life

"I do not encourage visitors."

—The Five Orange Pips

On the Disposing of Bodies

"The question now is, what shall we do with this poor wretch's body? We cannot leave it here to the foxes and the ravens."

—The Hound of the Baskervilles

His Brother's Quiet Place

"Very likely not. There are many men in London, you know, who, some from shyness, some from misanthropy, have no wish for the company of their fellows. Yet they are not averse to comfortable chairs and the latest periodicals. It is for the convenience of these that the Diogenes Club was started, and it now contains the most unsociable and unclubbable men in town. No member is permitted to take the least notice of any other one. Save in the Stranger's Room, no talking is, under any circumstances, allowed, and three offenses, if brought to the notice of the committee, render the talker liable to expulsion. My brother was one of the founders, and I have myself found it a very soothing atmosphere."

—The Greek Interpreter

The Fairer Sex, Advantages and Vexations

SIGNS OF A BROKEN HEART

"It is simplicity itself. When you bared your arm to draw that fish into the boat I saw that J. A. had been tattooed in the bend of the elbow. The letters were still legible, but it was perfectly clear from their blurred appearance, and from the staining of the skin round them, that efforts had been made to obliterate them. It was obvious, then, that those initials had once been very familiar to you, and that you had afterwards wished to forget them."

—*The "Gloria Scott"*

THAT SPECIAL ALLURE

"She is the daintiest thing under a bonnet on this planet."

—*A Scandal in Bohemia*

DANGEROUS WOMEN

"One of the most dangerous classes in the world's the drifting and friendless woman. She is the most harmless and often the most useful of mortals, but she is the inevitable inciter of crime in others. She is helpless. She is migratory. She has sufficient means to take her from country to country and from hotel to hotel. She is lost, as often as not, in a maze of obscure *pensions* and boarding-houses. She is a stray chicken in a world of foxes. When she is gobbled up she is hardly missed."

—The Disappearance of Lady Frances Carfax

DOMESTIC BLISS

"This is the Dundas separation case, and, as it happens, I was engaged in clearing up some small points in connection with it. The husband was a teetotaler, there was no other woman, and the conduct complained of was that he had drifted into the habit of winding up every meal by taking out his false teeth and hurling them at his wife, which, you will allow, is not an action likely to occur to the imagination of the average story-teller."

—A Case of Identity

FINDING SINGLE LADIES

"There is one correspondent who is a sure draw, Watson. That is the bank. Single ladies must live, and their passbooks are compressed diaries."

—The Disappearance of Lady Frances Carfax

GIRLS AND NATURE

"It is part of the settled order of nature that such a girl should have followers."

—The Adventure of the Solitary Cyclist

WOMEN, AGITATED

"She has flown to tea as an agitated woman will."

—The Crooked Man

THE NATURAL NATURE OF WOMEN

"Women are naturally secretive, and they like to do their own secreting."

—A Scandal in Bohemia

WIVES AND DEAD HUSBANDS

"I am not a whole-souled admirer of womankind . . . but my experience of life has taught me that there are few wives, having any regard for their husbands, who would let any man's spoken word stand between them and that husband's dead body. Should I ever marry, Watson, I should hope to inspire my wife with some feeling which would prevent her from being walked off by a housekeeper when my corpse was lying within a few yards of her."

—The Valley of Fear

JOBS UNFIT FOR WOMEN

"I confess that it is not the situation which I should like to see a sister of mine apply for."

—The Adventure of the Copper Beeches

PERSONALITY

"The lady's charming personality must not be permitted to warp our judgment."

—The Adventure of the Abbey Grange

On Women and Latin Blood

"A woman of Spanish blood does not condone such an injury so lightly."

—The Hound of the Baskervilles

The Motives of Women

"And yet the motives of women are so inscrutable. You remember the woman at Margate whom I suspected for the same reason. No powder on her nose—that proved to be the correct solution. How can you build on such a quicksand? Their most trivial action may mean volumes, or their most extraordinary conduct may depend upon a hairpin or a curling tongs."

—The Adventure of the Second Stain

On Female Charms, Ignoring Them

"I assure you that the most winning woman I ever knew was hanged for poisoning three little children for their insurance-money, and the most repellent man of my acquaintance is a philanthropist who has spent nearly a quarter of a million upon the London poor."

—The Sign of Four

LOVE, LOST

"A man always finds it hard to realize that he may have finally lost a woman's love, however badly he may have treated her."

—*The Musgrave Ritual*

ON YOUNG LADIES WHO KNOCK PEOPLE UP

"Now, when young ladies wander about the metropolis at this hour of the morning, and knock sleepy people up out of their beds, I presume that it is something very pressing which they have to communicate."

—*The Adventure of the Speckled Band*

THE MIND OF A WOMAN

"I have seen too much not to know that the impression of a woman may be more valuable than the conclusion of an analytical reasoner."

—*The Man with the Twisted Lip*

WOMEN AND TELEGRAMS

"No woman would ever send a reply-paid telegram. She would have come."

—*The Adventure of Wisteria Lodge*

PATIENCE AFTER DINNER
"All my instincts tell me that she is in London, but as we have at present no possible means of telling where, we can only take the obvious steps, eat our dinner, and possess our souls in patience."

—*The Disappearance of Lady Frances Carfax*

WOMEN, TO TRUST OR NOT
"Women are never to be entirely trusted—not the best of them."

—*The Sign of Four*

WOMAN, WRONGED
"When a woman has been seriously wronged by a man she no longer oscillates, and the usual symptom is a broken bell wire."

—*A Case of Identity*

❧

His Methods

His Method's Foundation

"You know my method. It is founded upon the observation of trifles."

—*The Boscombe Valley Mystery*

Just an Ordinary Man

"A conjurer gets no credit when once he has explained his trick; and if I show you too much of my method of working, you will come to the conclusion that I am a very ordinary individual after all."

—*A Study in Scarlet*

Intuition and Knowledge

"Quite so. I have a kind of intuition that way. Now and again a case turns up which is a little more complex. Then I have to bustle about and see things with my own eyes. You see I have a lot of special knowledge which I apply to the problem, and which facilitates matters wonderfully. Those rules of deduction laid down in that article which aroused your scorn are invaluable to me in practical work. Observation with me is second nature."

—*A Study in Scarlet*

GOING WITH YOUR GUT

"See the value of imagination. It is the one quality which Gregory lacks. We imagined what might have happened, acted upon the supposition, and find ourselves justified. Let us proceed."

—*Silver Blaze*

FOOTPRINTS AND THE TELLING STATE OF THE HANDS

"Here is my monograph upon the tracing of footsteps, with some remarks upon the uses of plaster of Paris as a preserver of impresses. Here, too, is a curious little work upon the influence of a trade upon the form of the hand, with lithotypes of the hands of slaters, sailors, cork-cutters, compositors, weavers, and diamond-polishers. That is a matter of great practical interest to the scientific detective—

especially in cases of unclaimed bodies, or in discovering the antecedents of criminals. But I weary you with my hobby."

—*The Sign of Four*

Ashes

"I gathered up some scattered ash from the floor. It was dark in color and flaky—such an ash is only made by a Trichinopoly. I have made a special study of cigar ashes—in fact, I have written a monograph upon the subject. I flatter myself that I can distinguish at a glance the ash of any known brand either of cigar or of tobacco."

—*A Study in Scarlet*

The Harpoon Test

"Have you tried to drive a harpoon through a body? No? Tut, tut, my dear sir, you must really pay attention to these details."

—*The Adventure of Black Peter*

Simplicity Itself in a Few Brief Observations

"It is simplicity itself; my eyes tell me that on the inside of your left shoe, just where the firelight strikes it, the leather is scored by six almost parallel cuts. Obviously they have been caused by someone who has very carefully scraped round the edges of the sole in order to remove crusted mud from it. Hence, you see, my double deduction that you had been out in vile weather, and that you had a particularly malignant boot-slitting specimen of the London slavey. As to your practice, if a gentleman walks into my rooms smelling of iodoform, with a black mark of nitrate of silver upon his right forefinger, and a bulge on the right side of his top-hat to show where he has secreted his stethoscope, I must be dull, indeed, if I do not pronounce him to be an active member of the medical profession."

—*A Scandal in Bohemia*

Suspicions First

"Let us hear the suspicions. I will look after the proofs."

—*The Adventure of the Three Students*

Planning Is Critical

"One should always look for a possible alternative, and provide against it. It is the first rule of criminal investigation."

—*The Adventure of Black Peter*

No Time to Explain

"I have no desire to make mysteries, but it is impossible at the moment of action to enter into long and complex explanations."

—*The Adventure of the Dancing Men*

Zen Mind, Beginner's Mind

"We approached the case, you remember, with an absolutely blank mind, which is always an advantage. We had formed no theories. We were simply there to observe and to draw inferences from our observations."

—*The Adventure of the Cardboard Box*

Finding a Starting Point

"There's plenty of thread, no doubt, but I can't get the end of it into my hand. Now, I'll state the case clearly and concisely, and maybe you can see a spark where all is dark to me."

—*The Man with the Twisted Lip*

The Unusual

"I love all that is bizarre and outside the conventions and humdrum routine of everyday life. You have shown your relish for it by the enthusiasm which has prompted you to chronicle, and, if you will excuse my saying so, somewhat to embellish so many of my own little adventures."

—*The Red-Headed League*

NOTES, THE VALUE OF COMPARING

"Oh, you must not let me influence you in any way. I suggest that you go on your line and I on mine. We can compare notes afterwards, and each will supplement the other."

—*The Adventure of the Six Napoleons*

PAPER CLUES

"I was hoping that if the paper on which he wrote was thin, some trace of it might come through upon this polished surface. No, I see nothing. I don't think there is anything more to be learned here. Now for the central table. This small pellet is, I presume, the black, doughy mass you spoke of. Roughly pyramidal in shape and hollowed out, I perceive. As you say, there appears to be grains of sawdust in it. Dear me, this is very interesting. And the cut—a positive tear, I see. It began with a thin scratch and ended in a jagged hole. I am much indebted to you for directing my attention to this case, Mr. Soames. Where does that door lead to?"

—*The Adventure of the Three Students*

On the Scent

"There are seventy-five perfumes, which it is very necessary that a criminal expert should be able to distinguish from each other, and cases have more than once within my own experience depended upon their prompt recognition."

—*The Hound of the Baskervilles*

On Shadowing Cabs

"On observing the cab I should have instantly turned and walked in the other direction. I should then at my leisure have hired a second cab and followed the first at a respectable distance, or, better still, have driven to the Northumberland Hotel and waited there."

—*The Hound of the Baskervilles*

Sherlock Holmes's Test

"Criminal cases are continually hinging upon that one point. A man is suspected of a crime months perhaps after it has been committed. His linen or clothes are examined and brownish stains discovered upon them. Are they blood stains, or mud stains, or rust stains, or fruit stains, or what are they? That is a question which has puzzled many an expert, and why? Because there was no reliable test. Now we have the Sherlock Holmes's test, and there will no longer be any difficulty."

—*A Study in Scarlet*

TOTAL DISCLOSURE

"I am afraid that my explanation may disillusion you, but it has always been my habit to hide none of my methods, either from my friend Watson or from anyone who might take an intelligent interest in them."

—*The Reigate Puzzle*

HIS SECRET DESIRE

"I have always had an idea that I would have made a highly efficient criminal. This is the chance of my lifetime in that direction. See here! This is a first-class, up-to-date burgling kit, with nickel-plated jimmy, diamond-tipped glass-cutter, adaptable keys, and every modern improvement which the march of civilization demands. Here, too, is my dark lantern. Everything is in order. Have you a pair of silent shoes?"

—The Adventure of Charles Augustus Milverton

On Reverting to Type

"Tomorrow it will be but a dreadful memory. With my hair cut and a few other superficial changes I shall no doubt reappear at Claridge's tomorrow as I was before this American stunt. Watson, my well of English seems to be permanently defiled—before this American job came my way."

—His Last Bow

False Beards

"And so could I—from which I gather that in all probability it was a false one. A clever man upon so delicate an errand has no use for a beard save to conceal his features."

—The Hound of the Baskervilles

ACTING, METHOD
"The best way of successfully acting a part is to be it."

—The Adventure of the Dying Detective

TRIPPING INTO THE NET
"But at last he made a trip—only a little, little trip—but it was more than he could afford, when I was so close upon him. I had my chance, and, starting from that point, I have woven my net round him until now it is all ready to close."

—The Final Problem

A PISTOL IN HIS POCKET
"The fact is that upon his entrance I had instantly recognized the extreme personal danger in which I lay. The only conceivable escape for him lay in silencing my tongue. In an instant I had slipped the revolver from the drawer into my pocket and was covering him through the cloth. At his remark I drew the weapon out and laid it cocked upon the table. He still smiled and blinked, but there was something about his eyes which made me feel very glad that I had it there."

—The Final Problem

THE MOTHER OF TRUTH

"And yet there should be no combination of events for which the wit of man cannot conceive an explanation. Simply as a mental exercise, without any assertion that it is true, let me indicate a possible line of thought. It is, I admit, mere imagination; but how often is imagination the mother of truth?"

—*The Valley of Fear*

Human, All Too Human

JEALOUSY
"They are as jealous as a pair of professional beauties."

—A Study in Scarlet

MIND THE STEP
"So you see our savage friend was very orthodox in his ritual. It is grotesque, Watson, but, as I have had occasion to remark, there is but one step from the grotesque to the horrible."

—The Adventure of Wisteria Lodge

LAUGHTER
"I can afford to laugh, because I know I will be even with them in the long run."

—A Study in Scarlet

Harmless Fellows

"He is a harmless enough fellow, Parker by name, a garroter by trade, and a remarkable performer on the jew's-harp."

—*The Adventure of the Empty House*

Good Lads

"You owe a very humble apology to that noble lad, your son, who has carried himself in this matter as I should be proud to see my own son do, should I ever chance to have one."

—*The Adventure of the Beryl Coronet*

Laziness, Curse of

"I am the most incurably lazy devil that ever stood in shoe leather— that is, when the fit is on me, for I can be spry enough at times."

—*A Study in Scarlet*

Reincarnation

"A study of family portraits is enough to convert a man to the doctrine of reincarnation."

—*The Hound of the Baskervilles*

Horsey Men

"There is a wonderful sympathy and freemasonry among horsey men. Be one of them and you will know all that there is to know."

—*A Scandal in Bohemia*

Life and Life Only

THE MEANING OF LIFE

"Life is infinitely stranger than anything which the mind of man could invent. We would not dare to conceive the things which are really mere commonplaces of existence. If we could fly out of that window hand in hand, hover over this great city, gently remove the roofs, and peep in at the queer things which are going on, the strange coincidences, the plannings, the cross-purposes, the wonderful chains of events, working through generations, and leading to the most *outré* results, it would make all fiction with its conventionalities and foreseen conclusions most stale and unprofitable."

—*A Case of Identity*

GETTING COMFORTABLE

"Now draw up and warm your toes. Here's a cigar, and the doctor has a prescription containing hot water and a lemon, which is good medicine on a night like this. It must be something important which has brought you out in such a gale."

—*The Adventure of the Golden Pince-Nez*

IMPORTANT MOMENTS

"Now is the dramatic moment of fate, when you hear a step upon the stair which is walking into your life, and you know not whether for good or ill."

—*The Hound of the Baskervilles*

ESCAPING THE COMMONPLACE

"I already feel it closing in upon me. My life is spent in one long effort to escape from the commonplaces of existence. These little problems help me to do so."

—*The Red-Headed League*

EXISTENCE, THE DULL ROUTINE OF

"I abhor the dull routine of existence. I crave for mental exaltation. That is why I have chosen my own particular profession, or rather created it, for I am the only one in the world."

—*The Sign of Four*

INTERRUPTIONS, TRIFLING

"This may be some trifling intrigue and I cannot break my other important research for the sake of it."

—*The Adventure of the Solitary Cyclist*

INSOMNIA NOW

"Do not go asleep, your very life may depend upon it. Have your pistol ready in case we should need it. I will sit on the side of the bed, and you in that chair."

—*The Adventure of the Speckled Band*

THE PERENNIAL PROBLEM

"What object is served by this circle of misery and violence and fear? It must tend to some end, or else our universe is ruled by chance, which is unthinkable. But what end? There is the great standing perennial problem to which human reason is as far from an answer as ever."

—*The Adventure of the Cardboard Box*

Stranger than Fiction

"For strange effects and extraordinary combinations we must go to life itself, which is always far more daring than any effort of the imagination."

—The Red-Headed League

Mediocrity Knows Nothing

"Mediocrity knows nothing higher than itself; but talent instantly recognizes genius."

—The Valley of Fear

On the Vapidity of Daily Existence

"Life is commonplace; the papers are sterile; audacity and romance seem to have passed forever from the criminal world."

—The Adventure of Wisteria Lodge

Floral Matters

"There is nothing in which deduction is so necessary as in religion. It can be built up as an exact science by the reasoner. Our highest assurance of the goodness of Providence seems to me to rest in the flowers. All other things, our powers, our desires, our food, are all really necessary for our existence in the first instance. But this rose is an extra. Its smell and its color are an embellishment of life, not a condition of it. It is only goodness which gives extras, and so I say again that we have much to hope from the flowers."

—*The Naval Treaty*

Mind Games

CONCENTRATION

"Intense mental concentration has a curious way of blotting out what has passed. The barrister who has his case at his fingers' ends and is able to argue with an expert upon his own subject finds that a week or two of the courts will drive it all out of his head once more."

—*The Hound of the Baskervilles*

BACKWARD REASONING MADE EASY

"Let me see if I can make it clearer. Most people, if you describe a train of events to them, will tell you what the result would be. They can put those events together in their minds, and argue from them that something will come to pass. There are few people, however, who, if you told them a result, would be able to evolve from their own inner consciousness what the steps were which led up to that result. This power is what I mean when I talk of reasoning backward, or analytically."

—*A Study in Scarlet*

AFGHANISTAN, THE TRAIN OF THOUGHT TO

"Nothing of the sort. I knew you came from Afghanistan. From long habit the train of thoughts ran so swiftly through my mind that I arrived at the conclusion without being conscious of intermediate steps. There were such steps, however. The train of reasoning ran, 'Here is a gentleman of a medical type, but with the air of a military man. Clearly an army doctor, then. He has just come from the tropics, for his face is dark, and that is not the natural tint of his skin, for his wrists are fair. He has undergone hardship and sickness, as his haggard face says clearly. His left arm has been injured. He holds it in a stiff and unnatural manner. Where in the tropics could an English army doctor have seen much hardship and got his arm wounded? Clearly in Afghanistan.' The whole train of thought did not occupy a second. I then remarked that you came from Afghanistan, and you were astonished."

—*A Study in Scarlet*

The Dangers of Premature Theorization

"The temptation to form premature theories upon insufficient data is the bane of our profession. I can see only two things for certain at present—a great brain in London, and a dead man in Sussex. It's the chain between that we are going to trace."

—The Valley of Fear

Conclusions, How to Get to One

"I reached this one by sitting upon five pillows and consuming an ounce of shag."

—The Man with the Twisted Lip

The Analytical Mind, Advantages of

"I have already explained to you that what is out of the common is usually a guide rather than a hindrance. In solving a problem of this sort, the grand thing is to be able to reason backward. That is a very useful accomplishment, and a very easy one, but people do not practice it much. In the everyday affairs of life it is more useful to reason forward, and so the other comes to be neglected. There are fifty who can reason synthetically for one who can reason analytically."

—A Study in Scarlet

GUESSING?

"No, no: I never guess. It is a shocking habit—destructive to the logical faculty. What seems strange to you is only so because you do not follow my train of thought or observe the small facts upon which large inferences may depend."

—*The Sign of Four*

PROGNOSTICATION

"It is a formidable difficulty, and I fear that you ask too much when you expect me to solve it. The past and the present are within the field of my inquiry, but what a man may do in the future is a hard question to answer."

—*The Hound of the Baskervilles*

BREAKING CODES

"I am fairly familiar with all forms of secret writings, and am myself the author of a trifling monograph upon the subject, in which I analyze one hundred and sixty separate ciphers, but I confess that this is entirely new to me. The object of those who invented the system has apparently been to conceal that these characters convey a message, and to give the idea that they are the mere random sketches of children.

"Having once recognized, however, that the symbols stood for letters, and having applied the rules which guide us in all forms of secret writings, the solution was easy enough.

"The first message submitted to me was so short that it was impossible for me to do more than to say, with some confidence, that the symbol of the stickman with both arms extended up in the air stood for E. As you are aware, E is the most common letter in the English alphabet, and it predominates to so marked an extent that even in a short sentence one would expect to find it most often. Out of fifteen symbols in the first message, four were the same, so it was reasonable to set this down as E."

—*The Adventure of the Dancing Men*

CIPHERS AND BOOKS

"Because there are many ciphers which I would read as easily as I do the apocrypha of the agony column: such crude devices amuse the intelligence without fatiguing it. But this is different. It is clearly a reference to the words in a page of some book. Until I am told which page and which book I am powerless."

—*The Valley of Fear*

CONJECTURE

"My dear Watson, there we come into those realms of conjecture where the most logical mind may be at fault."

—*The Adventure of the Empty House*

INFERENCE

"One true inference invariably suggests others."

—*Silver Blaze*

GETTING A HANDLE ON THE WEIRD

"The more *outré* and grotesque an incident is the more carefully it deserves to be examined, and the very point which appears to complicate a case is, when duly considered and scientifically handled, the one which is most likely to elucidate it."

—*The Hound of the Baskervilles*

ILLUSION OF GENIUS

"It is not really difficult to construct a series of inferences, each dependent upon its predecessor and each simple in itself. If, after doing so, one simply knocks out all the central inferences and presents one's audience with the starting-point and the conclusion, one may produce a startling, though possibly a meretricious, effect."

—The Adventure of the Dancing Men

On Mental Furniture

"I say now, as I said then, that a man should keep his little brain-attic stocked with all the furniture that he is likely to use, and the rest he can put away in the lumber-room of his library, where he can get it if he wants it."

—The Five Orange Pips

Mistakes Were Made

His Brains, Missing

"What has become of any brains that God has given me?"

—*The Disappearance of Lady Frances Carfax*

Blunder of a Lifetime

"How slow-witted I have been, and how nearly I have committed the blunder of my lifetime!"

—*The Adventure of the Abbey Grange*

Common Blunderer

"Because I made a blunder, my dear Watson—which is, I am afraid, a more common occurrence that anyone would think who only knew me through your memoirs."

—*Silver Blaze*

THE DANGER OF ENEMIES

"So long as he was free in London, my life would really not have been worth living. Night and day the shadow would have been over me, and sooner or later his chance must have come. What could I do? I could not shoot him at sight, or I should myself be in the dock. There was no use appealing to a magistrate. They cannot interfere on the strength of what would appear to them to be a wild suspicion."

—The Adventure of the Empty House

THE DEPENDABILITY OF JUSTICE

"Many a man has been wrongfully hanged."

—The Boscombe Valley Mystery

DISSIPATION

"Yes, I have been using myself up rather too freely. I have been a little pressed of late. Have you any objection to my closing your shutters?"

—The Final Problem

Error, Human

"It is human to err, and at least no one can accuse you of being a callous criminal."

—The Adventure of the Three Students

Errors of the Narrative Method

"You have erred, perhaps, in attempting to put color and life into each of your statements instead of confining yourself to the task of placing upon record that severe reasoning from cause to effect which is really the only notable feature about the thing."

—The Adventure of the Copper Beeches

Fate

"God help us! Why does fate play such tricks with poor, helpless worms? I never heard of such a case as this that I do not think of Baxter's words, and say, 'There, but for the grace of God, goes Sherlock Holmes.'"

—The Boscombe Valley Mystery

LAW, GETTING ON THE WRONG SIDE OF
"Legally, we are putting ourselves hopelessly in the wrong, but I think that it is worth it."

—The Yellow Face

HIS LIMITATIONS
"There is material here. There is scope. I am dull indeed not to have understood its possibilities."

—The Adventure of the Bruce-Partington Plans

OUT OF HIS KEN
"There is a realm in which the most acute and most experienced of detectives is helpless."

—The Hound of the Baskervilles

TAKING THINGS FOR GRANTED
"If I had not taken things for granted, if I had approached everything with care which I should have shown had we approached the case *de novo* and had no cut-and-dried story to warp my mind, should I not then have found something more definite to go upon?"

—The Adventure of the Abbey Grange

Temporary Eclipses of Sanity

"Should you care to add the case to your annals, my dear Watson, it can only be as an example of that temporary eclipse to which even the best-balanced mind may be exposed. Such slips are common to all mortals, and the greatest is he who can recognize and repair them."

—*The Disappearance of Lady Frances Carfax*

Alas

"Our birds are flown and the nest empty."

—*The Greek Interpreter*

Fitful Light

"I see some light in the darkness, but it may possibly flicker out."

—*The Adventure of the Bruce-Partington Plans*

Fool, Absolute

"I think, Watson, that you are now standing in the presence of one of the absolute fools in Europe."

—*The Man with the Twisted Lip*

On Keeping a Humble Attitude

"Watson, if it should ever strike you that I am getting a little over-confident in my powers, or giving less pains to a case than it deserves, kindly whisper 'Norbury' in my ear, and I shall be infinitely obliged to you."

—*The Yellow Face*

On the Correct Order of Fact and Theory

"It is a capital mistake to theorize in advance of the facts."

—*The Adventure of the Second Stain*

The Firm

THE STATE OF THE AGENCY

"But, indeed, if you are trivial, I cannot blame you, for the days of the great cases are past. Man, or at least criminal man, has lost all enterprise and originality. As to my own little practice, it seems to be degenerating into an agency for recovering lost lead pencils and giving advice to young ladies from boarding-schools."

—The Adventure of the Copper Beeches

WHAT TO WEAR

"We want overcoats and cravats and goulashes, and every aid that man ever invented to fight the weather."

—The Adventure of the Golden Pince-Nez

CLIENTS, STATUS OF

"I assure you, without affectation, that the status of my client is a matter of less moment to me than the interest of his case."

—*The Adventure of the Noble Bachelor*

CLIENTS, ROLE OF

"A client is to me a mere unit, a factor in a problem."

—*The Sign of Four*

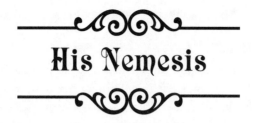

His Nemesis

THE NAPOLEON OF CRIME

"He is the Napoleon of crime, Watson. He is the organizer of half that is evil and of nearly all that is undetected in this great city. He is a genius, a philosopher, an abstract thinker. He has a brain of the first order."

—The Final Problem

ON HIS HIGHEST CALLING

"Ay, there's the genius and the wonder of the thing. The man pervades London, and no one has heard of him. That's what puts him on a pinnacle in the records of crime. I tell you, in all seriousness, that if I could beat that man, if I could free society of him, I should feel that my own career had reached its summit, and I should be prepared to turn to some more placid line in life."

—The Final Problem

The Professor Described

"His appearance was quite familiar to me. He is extremely tall and thin, his forehead domes out in a white curve, and his two eyes are deeply sunken in his head. He is clean-shaven, pale, and ascetic-looking, retaining something of the professor in his features. His shoulders are rounded from much study, and his face protrudes forward and is forever slowly oscillating from side to side in a curiously reptilian fashion. He peered at me with great curiosity in his puckered eyes."

—*The Final Problem*

The Résumé of Nemesis

"His career has been an extraordinary one. He is a man of good birth and excellent education, endowed by nature with a phenomenal mathematical faculty. At the age of twenty-one he wrote a treatise upon the binomial theorem, which has had a European vogue. On the strength of it he won the mathematical chair at one of our smaller universities, and had, to all appearances, a most brilliant career before him. But the man had hereditary tendencies of the most diabolical kind. A criminal strain ran in his blood, which, instead of being modified, was increased and rendered infinitely more dangerous by his extraordinary mental powers. Dark rumors gathered round him in the university town, and eventually he was compelled to resign his chair and to come down to London, where he set up as an army coach."

—The Final Problem

A Worthy Opponent

"You know my powers, my dear Watson, and yet at the end of three months I was forced to confess that I had at last met an antagonist who was my intellectual equal. My horror at his crimes was lost in my admiration of his skill."

—The Final Problem

Mission Impossible

"But the professor was fenced round with safeguards so cunningly devised that, do what I would, it seemed impossible to get evidence which would convict in a court of law."

—The Final Problem

The Trial of the Century

"In three days—that is to say, on Monday next—matters will be ripe, and the professor, with all the principal members of his gang, will be in the hands of the police. Then will come the greatest criminal trial of the century, the clearing up of over forty mysteries, and the rope for all of them; but if we move at all prematurely, you understand, they may slip out of our hands even at the last moment."

—The Final Problem

The Endgame

"Now, if I could have done this without the knowledge of Professor Moriarty, all would have been well. But he was too wily for that. He saw every step which I took to draw my coils round him. Again and again he strove to break away, but I as often headed him off."

—The Final Problem

The Number-One Contest in History

"I tell you, my friend, that if a detailed account of that silent contest could be written, it would take its place as the most brilliant bit of thrust-and-parry work in the history of detection. Never have I risen to such a height, and never have I been so hard pressed by an opponent. He cut deep, and yet I just undercut him. This morning the last steps were taken, and three days only were wanted to complete the business. I was sitting in my room thinking the matter over when the door opened and Professor Moriarty stood before me."

—*The Final Problem*

His Nemesis's Voice

"That was my singular interview with Professor Moriarty. I confess that it left an unpleasant effect upon my mind. His soft, precise fashion of speech leaves a conviction of sincerity which a mere bully could not produce. Of course, you will say: 'Why not take police precautions against him?' The reason is that I am well convinced that it is from his agents the blow would fall. I have the best of proofs that it would be so."

—*The Final Problem*

Never Underestimate

"My dear Watson, you evidently did not realize my meaning when I said that this man may be taken as being quite on the same intellectual plane as myself. You do not imagine that if I were the pursuer I should allow myself to be baffled by so slight an obstacle. Why, then, should you think so meanly of him?"

—*The Final Problem*

MORIARTY, GENIUS OF

"But in calling Moriarty a criminal you are uttering libel in the eyes of the law—and there lie the glory and the wonder of it! The greatest schemer of all time, the organizer of every deviltry, the controlling brain of the underworld, a brain which might have made or marred the destiny of nations—that's the man! But so aloof is he from general suspicion, so immune from criticism, so admirable in his management and self-effacement, that for those very words that you have uttered he could hale you to a court and emerge with your year's pension as a solatium for his wounded character. Is he not the celebrated author of *The Dynamics of an Asteroid*, a book which ascends to such rarefied heights of pure mathematics that it is said that there was no man in the scientific press capable of criticizing it? Is this a man to traduce? Foul-mouthed doctor and slandered professor—such would be your respective roles! That's genius, Watson. But if I am spared by lesser men, our day will surely come."

—*The Valley of Fear*

SINISTER, IN THE HIGHEST DEGREE

"Porlock, Watson, is a nom-de-plume, a mere identification mark; but behind it lies a shifty and evasive personality. In a former letter he frankly informed me that the name was not his own, and defied me ever to trace him among the teeming millions of this great city. Porlock is important, not for himself, but for the great man with whom he is in touch. Picture to yourself the pilot fish with the shark, the jackal with the lion—anything that is insignificant in companionship with what is formidable: not only formidable, Watson, but sinister—in the highest degree sinister. That is where he comes within my purview. You have heard me speak of Professor Moriarty?"

—The Valley of Fear

POWERS OF DARKNESS AND POSSIBILITIES

"When you have one of the first brains of Europe up against you, and all the powers of darkness at his back, there are infinite possibilities."

—The Valley of Fear

REPORTS OF MY DEATH . . .

"It came about in this way. The instant that the Professor had disappeared, it struck me what a really extraordinarily lucky chance Fate had placed in my way. I knew that Moriarty was not the only man who had sworn my death. There were at least three others whose desire for vengeance upon me would only be increased by the death of their leader. They were all most dangerous men. One or other would certainly get me. On the other hand, if all the world was convinced that I was dead they would take liberties, these men, they would soon lay themselves open, and sooner or later I could destroy them. Then it would be time for me to announce that I was still in the land of the living. So rapidly does the brain act that I believe I had thought this all out before Professor Moriarty had reached the bottom of the Reichenbach Falls."

—*The Adventure of the Empty House*

THE LAMENTED PASSING OF PROFESSOR MORIARTY

"The community is certainly the gainer, and no one the loser, save the poor out-of-work specialist, whose occupation has gone. With that man in the field, one's morning paper presented infinite possibilities. Often it was only the smallest trace, the faintest indication, and yet it was enough to tell me that the great malignant brain was there, as the gentlest tremors of the edges of the web remind one of the foul spider which lurks in the center. Petty thefts, wanton assaults, purposeless outrage—to the man who held the clue all could be worked into one connected whole. To the scientific student of the higher criminal world, no capital in Europe offered the advantages which London then possessed. But now. . ."

—*The Adventure of the Norwood Builder*

Just the Facts, Please

Just the Facts

"On the face of it the case is not a very complex one, though it certainly presents some novel and interesting features. A further knowledge of facts is necessary before I would venture to give a final and definite opinion."

—*The Adventure of Wisteria Lodge*

Gleaning the Essentials

"Of all the facts presented to us we had to pick just those which we deemed to be essential, and then piece them together in their order, so as to reconstruct this very remarkable chain of events."

—*The Naval Treaty*

THE NECESSITY OF DISCRIMINATION

"It is of the highest importance in the art of detection to be able to recognize, out of a number of facts, which are incidental and which vital. Otherwise your energy and attention must be dissipated instead of being concentrated."

—The Reigate Puzzle

ONLY THE OBVIOUS

"Beyond the obvious facts that he has at some time done manual labor, that he takes snuff, that he is a Freemason, that he has been in China, and that he has done a considerable amount of writing lately, I can deduce nothing else."

—The Red-Headed League

SIFTING THE FACTS

"Having gathered these facts, I smoked several pipes over them, trying to separate those which were crucial from others which were merely incidental."

—The Crooked Man

The Uses of All Knowledge

"All knowledge comes useful to the detective. Even the trivial fact that in the year 1865 a picture by Greuze entitled *La Jeune Fille a l'Agneau* fetched one million two hundred thousand francs—more than forty thousand pounds—at the Portalis sale may start a train of reflection in your mind."

—*The Valley of Fear*

On Being Led

"Now, I make a point of never having any prejudices, and of following docilely wherever fact may lead me."

—*The Reigate Puzzle*

The Secrets of Baker Street

"I was about to say that my friend and I have listened to a good many strange secrets in this room, and that we have had the good fortune to bring peace to many troubled souls. I trust that we may do as much for you. Might I beg you, as time may prove to be of importance, to furnish me with the facts of your case without further delay?"

—*The Yellow Face*

FACTS FIRST

"I will not bias your mind by suggesting theories or suspicions. I wish you simply to report facts in the fullest possible manner to me, and you can leave me to do the theorizing."

—*The Hound of the Baskervilles*

FAITH IN FACT

"I should have more faith. I ought to know by this time that when a fact appears to be opposed to a long train of deductions, it invariably proves to be capable of bearing some other interpretation."

—*A Study in Scarlet*

NOTHING IS OBVIOUSLY TRUE

"There is nothing more deceptive than an obvious fact."

—*The Boscombe Valley Mystery*

Good Beginnings

"Well, knowing as much as we do, it will be singular indeed if we fail to discover the rest. You must yourself have formed some theory which will explain the facts to which we have listened."

—*The Greek Interpreter*

At Leisure

RELAXATION AND FURNITURE
"No wind and not a cloud in the sky. I have a caseful of cigarettes here which need smoking, and the sofa is very much superior to the usual country hotel abomination."

—*The Boscombe Valley Mystery*

RELAXATION, HIS PREFERRED METHOD
"Well, I gave my mind a thorough rest by plunging into a chemical analysis. One of our greatest statesmen has said that a change of work is the best rest. So it is."

—*The Sign of Four*

His Retirement Project

"At present I am, as you know, fairly busy, but I propose to devote my declining years to the composition of a textbook which shall focus the whole art of detection into one volume."

—*The Adventure of the Abbey Grange*

The Stimulation of Work

"No: I am not tired. I have a curious constitution. I never remember feeling tired by work, though idleness exhausts me completely."

—*The Sign of Four*

Thinking of Goethe

"Yes, there are in me the makings of a very fine loafer, and also of a pretty spry sort of fellow. I often think of those lines of old Goethe: '*Schade dass die Natur nur einen Mensch aus dir schuf, Denn zum wurdigen Mann war und zum Schelmen der Stoff.*' "

—*The Sign of Four*

The Value of History

"It immensely adds to the zest of an investigation, my dear Mr. Mac, when one is in conscious sympathy with the historical atmosphere of one's surroundings."

—*The Valley of Fear*

A View of Sport

"My ramifications stretch out into many sections of society, but never, I am happy to say, into amateur sport, which is the best and soundest thing in England."

—*The Adventure of the Missing Three-Quarter*

Dinner, Late

"It is nearly nine, and the landlady babbled of green peas at seven-thirty."

—*The Adventure of the Three Students*

What He Did While Dead

"I traveled for two years in Tibet, therefore, and amused myself by visiting Lhassa, and spending some days with the head lama. You may have read of the remarkable explorations of a Norwegian named Sigerson, but I am sure that it never occurred to you that you were receiving news of your friend. I then passed through Persia, looked in at Mecca, and paid a short but interesting visit to the Khalifa at Khartoum, the results of which I have communicated to the Foreign Office. Returning to France, I spent some months in a research into the coal-tar derivatives, which I conducted in a laboratory at Montpellier, in the south of France."

—*The Adventure of the Empty House*

THE REMAINS OF THE DAY

"For me, there still remains the cocaine-bottle."

—*The Sign of Four*

WHEN TO STOP THINKING

"The thing takes shape. It becomes coherent. Might I ask you to hand me my violin, and we will postpone all further thought upon this business until the morning."

—*The Hound of the Baskervilles*

THE IMPORTANCE OF KNOWING PUGILISM

"I get so little active exercise that it is always a treat. You are aware that I have some proficiency in the good old British sport of boxing. Occasionally, it is of service; to-day, for example, I should have come to very ignominious grief without it."

—*The Adventure of the Solitary Cyclist*

HIS LATER WORKS

"Here is the fruit of my leisured ease, the magnum opus of my latter years, *Practical Handbook of Bee Culture, with Some Observations upon the Segregation of the Queen*. Alone I did it. Behold the fruit of pensive nights and laborious days when I watched the little working gangs as once I watched the criminal world of London."

—*His Last Bow*

THE POSITIVE SIDE OF COCAINE

"I suppose that its influence is physically a bad one. I find it, however, so transcendently stimulating and clarifying to the mind that its secondary action is a matter of small moment."

—*The Sign of Four*

Yet Another Small Weakness

"I suppose, that you imagine that I have added opium smoking to cocaine injections, and all the other little weaknesses on which you have favored me with your medical views."

—The Man with the Twisted Lip

The Ennui Perplex

"Draw your chair up and hand me my violin, for the only problem we have still to solve is how to while away these bleak autumnal evenings."

—The Adventure of the Noble Bachelor

Nature, Elemental Forces of

"How sweet the morning air is! See how that one little cloud floats like a pink feather from some gigantic flamingo. Now the red rim of the sun pushes itself over the London cloud-bank. It shines on a good many folk, but on none, I dare bet, who are on a stranger errand than you and I. How small we feel with our petty ambitions and strivings in the presence of the great elemental forces of Nature!"

—The Sign of Four

THE POST-PRANDIAL CONCERT
"And now for lunch, and then for Norman Neruda. Her attack and her bowing are splendid. What's that little thing of Chopin's she plays so magnificently: Tra-la-la-lira-lira-lay."

—*A Study in Scarlet*

DINING OUT
"When we have finished at the police-station I think that something nutritious at Simpson's would not be out of place."

—*The Adventure of the Dying Detective*

A NOBLE PURSUIT
"Meanwhile, we shall put the case aside until more accurate data are available, and devote the rest of our morning to the pursuit of Neolithic man."

—*The Adventure of the Devil's Foot*

Getting a Clue

UNIQUENESS
"Singularity is almost invariably a clue. The more featureless and commonplace a crime is, the more difficult it is to bring it home."

—The Boscombe Valley Mystery

NOTHING IS FOREVER HIDDEN
"What one man can invent another can discover."

—The Adventure of the Dancing Men

UNSUSPECTED DEPTHS
"This writing is of extraordinary interest. These are much deeper waters than I had thought."

—The Reigate Puzzle

UP TO SCRATCH

"This is recent, quite recent. See how the brass shines where it is cut. An old scratch would be the same color as the surface. Look at it through my lens. There's the varnish, too, like earth on each side of a furrow."

—*The Adventure of the Golden Pince-Nez*

FOOTPRINTS

"There is no branch of detective science which is so important and so much neglected as the art of tracing footsteps."

—*A Study in Scarlet*

A BREATH OF FRESH AIR

"Let us walk along the cliffs together and search for flint arrows. We are more likely to find them than clues to this problem. To let the brain work without sufficient material is like racing an engine. It racks itself to pieces. The sea air, sunshine, and patience—all else will come."

—*The Adventure of the Devil's Foot*

C'est N'pas Juste une Pipe

"Pipes are occasionally of extraordinary interest. Nothing has more individuality, save perhaps watches and bootlaces. The indications here, however, are neither very marked nor very important. The owner is obviously a muscular man, left-handed, with an excellent set of teeth, careless in his habits, and with no need to practice economy."

—*The Yellow Face*

❦

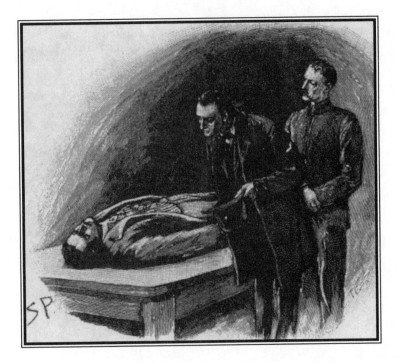

His Observations—
Mundane and Acute

THE SCIENCE OF DEDUCTION

"From a drop of water, a logician could infer the possibility of an Atlantic or a Niagara without having seen or heard of one or the other. So all life is a great chain, the nature of which is known whenever we are shown a single link of it. Like all other arts, the Science of Deduction and Analysis is one which can only be acquired by long and patient study, nor is life long enough to allow any mortal to attain the highest possible perfection in it. Before turning to those moral and mental aspects of the matter which present the greatest difficulties, let the inquirer begin by mastering more elementary problems. Let him, on meeting a fellow-mortal, learn at a glance to distinguish the history of the man, and the trade or profession to which he belongs. Puerile as such an exercise may seem, it sharpens the faculties of observation, and teaches one where to look and what to look for. By a man's finger-nails, by his coat-sleeve, by his boots, by his trouser knees, by the callosities of his forefinger and thumb, by his expression, by his shirt-cuffs—by each of these things a man's calling is plainly revealed. That all united should fail to enlighten the competent inquirer in any case is almost inconceivable."

—*A Study in Scarlet*

OBSERVATION, THE VALUE OF SIMPLE

"It is simplicity itself, so absurdly simple that an explanation is superfluous; and yet it may serve to define the limits of observation and of deduction. Observation tells me that you have a little reddish mold adhering to your instep. Just opposite the Wigmore Street Office they have taken up the pavement and thrown up some earth, which lies in such a way that it is difficult to avoid treading in it in entering. The earth is of this peculiar reddish tint which is found, as far as I know, nowhere else in the neighborhood. So much is observation. The rest is deduction."

—*The Sign of Four*

JEALOUSY, TRANSFORMING

"Jealousy is a strange transformer of characters."

—*The Adventure of the Noble Bachelor*

THE IMPORTANCE OF BEING SPECIFIC

"Never trust to general impressions, my boy, but concentrate yourself upon details."

—*A Case of Identity*

HOIST BY HIS OWN PETARD

"Violence does, in truth, recoil upon the violent and the schemer falls into the pit which he digs for another."

—*The Adventure of the Speckled Band*

THE DEPTH OF THE PARSLEY

"The affair seems absurdly trifling, and yet I dare call nothing trivial when I reflect that some of my most classic cases have had the least promising commencement. You will remember, Watson, how the dreadful business of the Abernetty family was first brought to my notice by the depth which the parsley had sunk into the butter upon a hot day."

—*The Adventure of the Six Napoleons*

THE HORROR, THE HORROR
"I can understand. There is a mystery about this which stimulates the imagination; where there is no imagination there is no horror. Have you seen the evening paper?"

—A Study in Scarlet

HUMAN NATURE
"What you do in this world is a matter of no consequence. The question is, what can you make people believe that you have done?"

—A Study in Scarlet

JOURNEYS
"Journeys end in lovers' meetings."

—The Adventure of the Empty House

INTELLECTUAL REACH
"One's ideas must be as broad as Nature if they are to interpret Nature."

—A Study in Scarlet

NIGHTWORK

"Moonshine is a brighter thing than fog."

—The Boscombe Valley Mystery

LITTLE THINGS

"It has long been an axiom of mine that the little things are infinitely the most important."

—A Case of Identity

MALINGERING, KNOWLEDGE OF

"Malingering is a subject upon which I have sometimes thought of writing a monograph."

—The Adventure of the Dying Detective

THE DEEPER MEANING OF EXPENSIVE TOBACCO

"This is Grosvenor mixture at eightpence an ounce. As he might get an excellent smoke for half the price, he has no need to practice economy."

—The Yellow Face

PACING ON THE PAVEMENT
"Oscillation upon the pavement always means an *affaire de coeur*."
—*A Case of Identity*

ON STATURE
"Why, the height of a man, in nine cases out of ten, can be told from the length of his stride. It is a simple calculation enough, though there is no use my boring you with figures. I had this fellow's stride both on the clay outside and on the dust within. Then I had a way of checking my calculation. When a man writes on a wall, his instinct leads him to write above the level of his own eyes. Now that writing was just over six feet from the ground. It was child's play."
—*A Study in Scarlet*

AN OBVIOUS FACT ABOUT THE EARS
"You have observed, of course, that the ears are not a pair."
—*The Adventure of the Cardboard Box*

SIGNS OF BEING SCARED

"Friend Porlock is evidently scared out of his senses—kindly compare the writing in the note to that upon its envelope, which was done, he tells us, before this ill-omened visit. The one is clear and firm. The other hardly legible."

—*The Valley of Fear*

FACTS ABOUT DEPTH

"You may have observed the same wheel-tracks going the other way. But the outward-bound ones were very much deeper—so much so that we can say for a certainty that there was a very considerable weight on the carriage."

—*The Greek Interpreter*

PIPES, DEDUCTIONS FROM

"He has been in the habit of lighting his pipe at lamps and gas-jets. You can see that it is quite charred all down one side. Of course a match could not have done that. Why should a man hold a match to the side of his pipe? But you cannot light it at a lamp without getting the bowl charred. And it is all on the right side of the pipe. From that I gather that he is a left-handed man. You hold your own pipe to the lamp and see how naturally you, being right-handed, hold the left side to the flame. You might do it once the other way, but not as a constancy. This has always been held so. Then he has bitten through his amber. It takes a muscular, energetic fellow, and one with a good set of teeth, to do that. But if I am not mistaken I hear him upon the stair, so we shall have something more interesting than his pipe to study."

—*The Yellow Face*

HANDICAPS

"He is a cripple in the sense that he walks with a limp; but in other respects he appears to be a powerful and well-nurtured man. Weakness in one limb is often compensated for by exceptional strength in the others."

—*The Man with the Twisted Lip*

UNTIDY ACTIVITIES

"If a herd of buffaloes had passed along, there could not be a greater mess."

—*A Study in Scarlet*

SINKING, OBVIOUS CLUES TO

"When water is near and a weight is missing it is not a very far-fetched supposition that something has been sunk in the water."

—*The Valley of Fear*

GLASSES, WHAT THEY SAY

"Surely my deductions are simplicity itself. It would be difficult to name any articles which afford a finer field for inference than a pair of glasses, especially so remarkable a pair as these. That they belong to a woman I infer from their delicacy, and also, of course, from the last words of the dying man. As to her being a person of refinement and well dressed, they are, as you perceive, handsomely mounted in solid gold, and it is inconceivable that anyone who wore such glasses could be slatternly in other respects. You will find that the clips are too wide for your nose, showing that the lady's nose was very broad at the base. This sort of nose is usually a short and coarse one, but there is a sufficient number of exceptions to prevent me from being dogmatic or from insisting upon this point in my description. My own face is a narrow one, and yet I find that I cannot get my eyes into the center, nor near the center, of these glasses. Therefore, the lady's eyes are set very near to the sides of the nose. You will perceive that the glasses are concave and of unusual strength. A lady whose vision has been so extremely contracted all her life is sure to have the physical characteristics of such vision, which are seen in the forehead, the eyelids, and the shoulders."

—The Adventure of the Golden Pince-Nez

KNOWING VS. EXPLAINING

"It was easier to know it than to explain why I know it. If you were asked to prove that two and two made four, you might find some difficulty, and yet you are quite sure of the fact. Even across the street I could see a great blue anchor tattooed on the back of the fellow's hand. That smacked of the sea. He had a military carriage, however, and regulation side whiskers. There we have the marine. He was a man with some amount of self-importance and a certain air of command. You must have observed the way in which he held his head and swung his cane. A steady, respectable, middle-aged man, too, on the face of him—all facts which led me to believe that he had been a sergeant."

—A Study in Scarlet

WHAT HE COULD TELL FROM A HAT

"It is perhaps less suggestive than it might have been, and yet there are a few inferences which are very distinct, and a few others which represent at least a strong balance of probability. That the man was highly intellectual is of course obvious upon the face of it, and also that he was fairly well-to-do within the last three years, although he has now fallen upon evil days. He had foresight, but has less now than formerly, pointing to a moral retrogression, which, when taken with the decline of his fortunes, seems to indicate some evil influence, probably drink, at work upon him. This may account also for the obvious fact that his wife has ceased to love him.

"He has, however, retained some degree of self-respect. He is a man who leads a sedentary life, goes out little, is out of training entirely, is middle-aged, has grizzled hair which he has had cut within the last few days, and which he anoints with lime-cream. These are the more patent facts which are to be deduced from his hat. Also, by the way, that it is extremely improbable that he has gas laid on in his house."

—The Adventures of the Blue Carbuncle

SURPRISED?

"Why should I be surprised? I receive an anonymous communication from a quarter which I know to be important, warning me that danger threatens a certain person. Within an hour I learn that this danger has actually materialized and that the person is dead. I am interested; but, as you observe, I am not surprised."

—*The Valley of Fear*

ONE IMPORTANT THING

"Only one important thing has happened in the last three days, and that is that nothing has happened."

—*The Adventure of the Second Stain*

FIRE AND THE SINGLE WOMAN

"When a woman thinks that her house is on fire, her instinct is at once to rush to the thing which she values most. It is a perfectly overpowering impulse, and I have more than once taken advantage of it. A married woman grabs at her baby; an unmarried one reaches for her jewel-box."

—*A Scandal in Bohemia*

SMELL

"Having sniffed the dead man's lips, I detected a slightly sour smell, and I came to the conclusion that he had had poison forced upon him."

—A Study in Scarlet

The Problem with Taking Trains

"According to my experience it is not possible to reach the platform of a Metropolitan train without exhibiting one's ticket."

—The Adventure of the Bruce-Partington Plans

History

"Now having secured the future, we can afford to be more lenient with the past."

—The Adventure of the Priory School

Tattoos

"The fish you have tattooed immediately above your right wrist could only have been done in China. I have made a small study of tattoo marks and have even contributed to the literature of the subject. That trick of staining the fishes' scales of a delicate pink is quite peculiar to China."

—The Red-Headed League

Thank You for Smoking

"I observe from your forefinger that you make your own cigarettes. Have no hesitation in lighting one."

—The Hound of the Baskervilles

Truth, Encore

"How often have I said to you that when you have eliminated the impossible, whatever remains, however improbable, must be the truth?"

—The Sign of Four

What We Can See from Maps

"Exactly, I fancy the yew alley, though not marked under that name, must stretch along this line, with the moor, as you perceive, upon the right of it. This small clump of buildings here is the hamlet of Grimpen, where our friend Dr. Mortimer has his headquarters. Within a radius of five miles there are, as you see, only a very few scattered dwellings. Here is Lafter Hall, which was mentioned in the narrative. There is a house indicated here which may be the residence of the naturalist—Stapleton, if I remember right, was his name. Here are two moorland farmhouses, High Tor and Foulmire.

Then fourteen miles away the great convict prison of Princetown. Between and around these scattered points extends the desolate, lifeless moor. This, then, is the stage upon which tragedy has been played, and upon which we may help to play it again."

—*The Hound of the Baskervilles*

WHERE TO LOOK

"You did not know where to look, and so you missed all that was important. I can never bring you to realize the importance of sleeves, the suggestiveness of thumb-nails, or the great issues that may hand from a boot-lace."

—*A Case of Identity*

THE FULLY FUNCTIONAL WALKING STICK

"You have a very handsome stick. By the inscription I observed that you had not had it more than a year. But you have taken some pains to bore the head of it and pour melted lead into the hole so as to make it a formidable weapon. I argued that you would not take such precautions unless you had some danger to fear."

—*The "Gloria Scott"*

Hats, What They Can Reveal

"If you wish to preserve your incognito, I would suggest that you cease to write your name upon the lining of your hat, or else that you turn the crown towards the person whom you are addressing."

—The Yellow Face

The Blindness of Sight

"You see, but you do not observe. The distinction is clear. For example, you have frequently seen the steps which lead up from the hall to this room."

—A Scandal in Bohemia

No Help from the Palace

"I'm afraid that all the queen's horses and all the queen's men cannot avail in this matter."

—The Adventure of the Bruce-Partington Plans

On Getting Sensitive Information from the Government

"There may be some disinclination on the part of the officials to oblige you. There is so much red tape in these matters. I have no doubt that with a little delicacy and finesse the end may be obtained."

—The Adventure of the Missing Three-Quarter

HISTORICAL CHANGE

"There's an east wind coming all the same, such a wind as never blew on England yet. It will be cold and bitter, and a good many of us may wither before its blast. But it's God's own wind none the less, and a cleaner, better, stronger land will lie in the sunshine when the storm has cleared."

—His Last Bow

BATTERIES, FEELINGS OF

"I wonder how a battery feels when it pours electricity into a non-conductor."

—The Adventure of the Dying Detective

The Proper Study of Mankind

The Joy of Americans

"It is always a joy to meet an American, for I am one of those who believe that the folly of a monarch and the blundering of a minister in far-gone years will not prevent our children from being some day citizens of the same world-wide country under a flag which shall be a quartering of the Union Jack with the Stars and Stripes."

—The Adventure of the Noble Bachelor

Appearances, Keeping Them Up

"He's a fine fellow. But he has a struggle to keep up his position. He is far from rich, and has many calls. You noticed, of course, that his boots had been re-soled."

—The Naval Treaty

THE ARMCHAIR DETECTIVE

"I said that he was my superior in observation and deduction. If the art of the detective began and ended in reasoning from an armchair, my brother would be the greatest criminal agent that ever lived. But he has no ambition and no energy. He will not even go out of his way to verify his own solutions, and would rather be considered wrong than take the trouble to prove himself right. Again and again I have taken a problem to him, and have received an explanation which has afterwards proved to be the correct one. And yet he was absolutely incapable of working out the practical points which must be gone into before a case could be laid before a judge or jury."

—The Greek Interpreter

ATHLETES AND DUMB-BELLS, SHOCKING PICTURES OF

"Dear me, Watson, is it possible that you have not penetrated the fact that the case hangs upon the missing dumb-bell? Well, well, you need not be downcast, for between ourselves I don't think that either Inspector Mac or the excellent local practitioner has grasped the overwhelming importance of this incident. One dumb-bell, Watson! Consider an athlete with one dumb-bell! Picture to yourself the unilateral development, the imminent danger of a spinal curvature. Shocking, Watson, shocking!"

—*The Valley of Fear*

On Being a Fisher of Men

"The nets are all in place, and the drag is about to begin. We'll know before the day is out whether we have caught our big, lean-jawed pike, or whether he has got through the meshes."

—*The Hound of the Baskervilles*

Big Toes and Religion

"The Hindoo proper has long and thin feet. The sandal-wearing Mohammedan has the great toe well separated from the others because the thong is commonly passed between."

—*The Sign of Four*

British Workmen

"Sorry to see that you've had the British workman in the house. He's a token of evil."

—*The Crooked Man*

On Checking with the Roommate

"That's good enough. I generally have chemicals about, and occasionally do experiments. Would that annoy you?"

—*A Study in Scarlet*

Closing In

"We have him, we have him and I dare swear that before to-morrow night he will be fluttering in our net as helpless as one of his own butterflies. A pin, a cork, and a card, and we add him to the Baker Street collection!"

—*The Hound of the Baskervilles*

A Clubbable Man

"The Diogenes Club is the queerest club in London, and Mycroft one of the queerest men. He's always there from quarter to five to twenty to eight. It's six now, so if you care for a stroll this beautiful evening I shall be very happy to introduce you to two curiosities."

—*The Greek Interpreter*

Insights Gleaned from Children

"I have frequently gained my first real insight into the character of parents by studying their children. This child's disposition is abnormally cruel, merely for cruelty's sake, and whether he derives this from his smiling father, as I should suspect, or from his mother, it bodes evil for the poor girl who is in their power."

—*The Adventure of the Copper Beeches*

Don't Rile the English

"The Englishman is a patient creature, but at present his temper is a little inflamed, and it would be as well not to try him too far."

—*His Last Bow*

Employees, Value of Disgruntled

"So much I learned partly from village gossip and partly from my own observation. There are no better instruments than discharged servants with a grievance, and I was lucky enough to find one."

—*The Adventure of Wisteria Lodge*

FACES AT THE WINDOW
"There is something very attractive about that livid face at the window."

—The Yellow Face

FALLING AND RISING
"For once you have fallen low. Let us see in the future how high you can rise."

—The Adventure of the Three Students

FINESSE, SURPRISING
"I knew that this man Small had a certain degree of low cunning, but I did not think him capable of anything in the nature of delicate finesse. That is usually a product of higher education."

—The Sign of Four

FOOLS
"Then he's no use to me. I'm a practical man."

—The Valley of Fear

An Insolent Man

"Fancy his having the insolence to confound me with the official detective force."

—*The Adventure of the Speckled Band*

Knees

"I hardly looked at his face. His knees were what I wished to see."

—*The Red-Headed League*

Lawyers, Abilities of

"A clever counsel would tear it all to rags."

—*Silver Blaze*

Lecoq

"Lecoq was a miserable bungler, he had only one thing to recommend him, and that was his energy. That book made me positively ill. The question was how to identify an unknown prisoner. I could have done it in twenty-four hours. Lecoq took six months or so. It might be made a textbook for detectives to teach them what to avoid."

—*A Study in Scarlet*

MYCROFT: THE ONE-MAN INTELLIGENCE AGENCY

"Well, his position is unique. He has made it for himself. There has never been anything like it before, nor will be again. He has the tidiest and most orderly brain, with the greatest capacity for storing facts, of any man living. The same great powers which I have turned to the detection of crime he has used for this particular business. The conclusions of every department are passed to him, and he is the central exchange, the clearing-house, which makes out the balance. All other men are specialists, but his specialism is omniscience. We will suppose that a minister needs information as to a point which involves the Navy, India, Canada and the bimetallic question; he could get his separate advices from various departments upon each, but only Mycroft can focus them all, and say offhand how each factor would affect the other. They began by using him as a short-cut, a convenience; now he has made himself an essential. In that great brain of his everything is pigeon-holed and can be handed out in an instant. Again and again his word has decided the national policy. He lives in it. He thinks of nothing else save when, as an intellectual exercise, he unbends if I call upon him and ask him to advise me on one of my little problems."

—*The Adventure of the Bruce-Partington Plans*

Night People

"Run down, my dear fellow, and open the door, for all virtuous folk have been long in bed."

—*The Adventure of the Golden Pince-Nez*

On Not Being Too Forthcoming

"The main thing with people of that sort is never to let them think that their information can be of the slightest importance to you. If you do they will instantly shut up like an oyster. If you listen to them under protest, as it were, you are very likely to get what you want."

—*The Sign of Four*

The Pain of Being Shorter

"I am glad to stretch myself, Watson. It is no joke when a tall man has to take a foot off his stature for several hours on end."

—*The Adventure of the Empty House*

Private Admissions

"He knows that I am his superior, and acknowledges it to me; but he would cut his tongue out before he would own it to any third person."

—*A Study in Scarlet*

THE QUALITY OF MERCY

"I am not retained by the police to supply their deficiencies. If Horner were in danger it would be another thing, but this fellow will not appear against him, and the case must collapse. I suppose that I am commuting a felony, but it is just possible that I am saving a soul. This fellow will not go wrong again; he is too terribly frightened. Send him to jail now, and you make him a jail-bird for life. Besides, it is the season of forgiveness. Chance has put in our way a most singular and whimsical problem, and its solution is its own reward."

—*The Adventure of the Blue Carbuncle*

A SHORT COMMUTE

"What is to me a means of livelihood is to him the merest hobby of a dilettante. He has an extraordinary faculty for figures, and audits the books in some of the government departments. Mycroft lodges in Pall Mall, and he walks round the corner into Whitehall every morning and back every evening. From year's end to year's end he takes no other exercise, and is seen nowhere else, except only in the Diogenes Club, which is just opposite his rooms."

—The Greek Interpreter

SLEEP OF THE STOUT
"On the other hand, like all these stout, little men who do themselves well, he is a plethoric sleeper."

—The Adventure of Charles Augustus Milverton

SMOKING COMPANIONS
"I should not sit here smoking with you if I thought that you were a common criminal, you may be sure of that."

—The Adventure of the Abbey Grange

ON TREES AND PEOPLE
"There are some trees, Watson, which grow to a certain height, and then suddenly develop some unsightly eccentricity. You will see it often in humans. I have a theory that the individual represents in his development the whole procession of his ancestors, and that such a sudden turn to good or evil stands for some strong influence which

came into the line of his pedigree. The person becomes, as it were, the epitome of the history of his own family."

—*The Adventure of the Empty House*

UNIVERSAL IMMORTAL SPARK

"Dirty-looking rascals, but I suppose every one has some little immortal spark concealed about him. You would not think it, to look at them. There is no a priori probability about it. A strange enigma is man!"

—*The Sign of Four*

VISAGE

"The features are given to man as the means by which he shall express his emotions, and yours are faithful servants."

—*The Adventure of the Cardboard Box*

WAGERING GENTLEMEN

"When you see a man with whiskers of that cut and the 'Pink 'un' protruding out of his pocket, you can always draw him by a bet. I daresay that if I had put £100 down in front of him, that man would not have given me such complete information as was drawn from him by the idea that he was doing me on a wager."

—*The Adventure of the Blue Carbuncle*

REALLY EVIL MEN

"Evil indeed is the man who has not one woman to mourn him."

—*The Hound of the Baskervilles*

CRANIAL CAPACITY

"It is a question of cubic capacity. A man with so large a brain must have something in it."

—*The Adventure of the Blue Carbuncle*

Police, Mostly Baffled

THE ADVANTAGE OF NOT BEING A POLICEMAN

"I follow my own methods and tell as much or as little as I choose. That is the advantage of being unofficial. I don't know whether you observed it, Watson, but the colonel's manner has been just a trifle cavalier to me. I am inclined now to have a little amusement at his expense. Say nothing to him about the horse."

—*Silver Blaze*

ADVICE TO A YOUNG POLICEMAN

"Out of my last fifty-three cases my name has only appeared in four, and the police have had the credit in forty-nine. I don't blame you for not knowing this, for you are young and inexperienced, but if you wish to get on in your new duties you will work with me and not against me."

—*The Naval Treaty*

His Method and the Police

"I go into a case to help the ends of justice and the work of the police. If I have ever separated myself from the official force, it is because they have first separated themselves from me. I have no wish ever to score at their expense. At the same time, Mr. White Mason, I claim the right to work in my own way and give my results at my own time—complete rather than in stages."

—*The Valley of Fear*

Getting Ahead at the Yard

"I have written to Lestrade asking him to supply us with the details which are now wanting, and which he will only get after he has secured his man. That he may be safely trusted to do, for although he is absolutely devoid of reason, he is as tenacious as a bulldog when he once understands what he has to do, and, indeed, it is just this tenacity which has brought him to the top at Scotland Yard."

—*The Adventure of the Cardboard Box*

Imagination, Lack of

"Inspector Gregory, to whom the case has been committed, is an extremely competent officer. Were he but gifted with imagination he might rise to great heights in his profession."

—Silver Blaze

INSTINCTS VS. FACTS

"All my instincts are one way, and all the facts are the other, and I much fear that British juries have not yet attained that pitch of intelligence when they will give the preference to my theories over Lestrade's facts."

—The Adventure of the Norwood Builder

THE NORMAL STATE OF THE POLICE

"When Gregson, or Lestrade, or Athelney Jones are out of their depths—which, by the way, is their normal state—the matter is laid before me."

—The Sign of Four

HELPING THE POLICE

"I shall be my own police. When I have spun the web they may take the flies, but not before."

—The Five Orange Pips

RURAL POLICE
"Local aid is always either worthless or else biased."

—The Boscombe Valley Mystery

THE STRENGTHS AND WEAKNESSES OF THE FRENCH
"I was consulted last week by Francois le Villard, who, as you probably know, has come rather to the front lately in the French detective service. He has all the Celtic power of quick intuition, but he is deficient in the wide range of exact knowledge which is essential to the higher developments of his art."

—The Sign of Four

SUPPRESSED EVIDENCE
"It is not for me, my dear Watson, to stand in the way of the official police force. I leave them all the evidence which I found."

—The Adventure of the Devil's Foot

THAT INFERIOR DUPIN
"Now, in my opinion, Dupin was a very inferior fellow. That trick of his of breaking in on his friends' thoughts with an apropos remark

after a quarter of an hour's silence is really very showy and superficial. He had some analytical genius, no doubt; but he was by no means such a phenomenon as Poe appeared to imagine."

—A Study in Scarlet

Two Out of Three

"He has considerable gifts himself. He possesses two out of the three qualities necessary for the ideal detective. He has the power of observation and that of deduction. He is only wanting in knowledge, and that may come in time. He is now translating my small works into French."

—The Sign of Four

Scorched Earth Investigators

"With two such men as yourself and Lestrade upon the ground, there will not be much for a third party to find out."

—A Study in Scarlet

The Scarlet Thread

MURDER RUNS THROUGH IT

"There's the scarlet thread of murder running through the colorless skein of life, and our duty is to unravel it, and isolate it, and expose every inch of it."

—A Study in Scarlet

WHAT IT IS

"It is murder, refined, cold-blooded, deliberate murder. Do not ask me for particulars. My nets are closing upon him, and he is already almost at my mercy. There is but one danger which can threaten us. It is that he should strike before we are ready to do so. Another day—two at the most—and I have my case complete, but until then guard your charge as closely as ever a fond mother watched her ailing child."

—The Hound of the Baskervilles

THE BLUE CARBUNCLE

"It's a bonny thing. Just see how it glints and sparkles. Of course it is a nucleus and focus of crime. Every good stone is. They are the devil's pet baits. In the larger and older jewels every facet may stand for a bloody deed. This stone is not yet twenty years old. It was found in the banks of the Amoy River in southern China and is remarkable in having every characteristic of the carbuncle, save that it is blue in shade instead of ruby red. In spite of its youth, it has already a sinister history. There have been two murders, a vitriol-throwing, a suicide, and several robberies brought about for the sake of this forty grain weight of crystallized charcoal. Who would think that so pretty a toy would be a purveyor to the gallows and the prison?"

—The Adventure of the Blue Carbuncle

THE EARS HAVE IT

"Bodies in the dissecting-rooms are injected with preservative fluid. These ears bear no signs of this. They are fresh, too. They have been cut off with a blunt instrument, which would hardly happen if a student had done it. Again, carbolic or rectified spirits would be the preservatives which would suggest themselves to the medical mind, certainly not rough salt. I repeat that there is no practical joke here, but that we are investigating a serious crime."

—*The Adventure of the Cardboard Box*

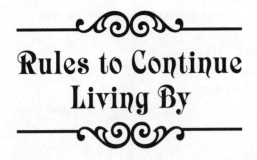

Rules to Continue Living By

Action
"You must act, man, or you are lost. Nothing but energy can save you. This is no time for despair."

—The Five Orange Pips

Assigned Tasks
"My dear fellow, you shall keep watch in the street. I'll do the criminal part."

—The Adventure of the Bruce-Partington Plans

Be Silent and See
"This is a time for observation, not for talk."

—The Red-Headed League

BETTER LATE THAN ...

"I confess that I have been as blind as a mole, but it is better to learn wisdom late than never to learn it at all."

—The Man with the Twisted Lip

CABS, RULES FOR TAKING THEM

"In the morning you will send for a hansom, desiring your man to take neither the first nor the second which may present itself."

—The Final Problem

CIGARETTES, HEALTH BENEFITS FOR

"Have a cigarette, Mr. McFarlane. Beyond obvious facts that you are an asthmatic, I know nothing whatever about you."

—The Adventure of the Norwood Builder

CONSCIENCE, LIGHT

"In this way I am no doubt responsible indirectly for Dr. Grimesby Roylott's death, and I cannot say that it is likely to weigh very heavily upon my conscience."

—The Adventure of the Speckled Band

CONTINUING EDUCATION

"Education never ends, Watson. It is a series of lessons with the greatest for the last."

—*The Adventure of the Red Circle*

CORRESPONDENCE, SCREENING

"My correspondence is a varied one and I am somewhat upon my guard against any packages which reach me."

—*The Adventure of the Dying Detective*

DANGER, WHAT DANGER?

"There is no prospect of danger, or I should not dream of stirring out without you."

—*The Adventure of the Norwood Builder*

EMOTIONS

"The emotional qualities are antagonistic to clear reasoning."

—*The Sign of Four*

EXCEPTIONS

"I never make exceptions. An exception disproves the rule."

—The Sign of Four

FINDING THE TRUTH

"Eliminate all other factors, and the one which remains must be the truth."

—The Sign of Four

HIGH STAKES

"You must play your cards as best you can when such a stake is on the table."

—The Adventure of Charles Augustus Milverton

LIABILITY

"I must take the view that when a man embarks upon a crime, he is morally guilty of any other crime which may spring from it."

—The Adventure of the Priory School

Not Too Quick

"Let us know a little more before we act."

—The Adventure of the Abbey Grange

The Obvious

"The world is full of obvious things which nobody by any chance ever observes."

—The Hound of the Baskervilles

Separation

"Let us try to realize what we do know, so as to make the most of it, and to separate the essential from the accidental."

—The Adventure of the Priory School

Significant Items

"I think anything out of the ordinary routine of life well worth reporting."

—The Hound of the Baskervilles

DON'T BE STUPID, BE PARANOID

"I think that you know me well enough to understand that I am by
no means a nervous man. At the same time, it is stupidity rather than
courage to refuse to recognize danger when it is close upon you."

—The Final Problem

PATIENCE, QUIET

"Let us possess our souls in patience and make as little noise as
possible."

—The Valley of Fear

PATIENT SOULS

"Well, we can only possess our souls in patience until this excellent
inspector comes back for us."

—The Adventure of Wisteria Lodge

PERSONALITIES PLEASE

"It is of the first importance not to allow your judgment to be biased
by personal qualities."

—The Sign of Four

PLODDING ON

"Every fresh advance which we make only reveals a fresh ridge beyond. And yet we have surely made some appreciable progress."

—*The Adventure of the Bruce-Partington Plans*

AGAINST PREMATURE ACTIONS

"If they are innocent it would be a cruel injustice, and if they are guilty we should be giving up all chance of bringing it home to them. No, no, we will preserve them upon our list of suspects."

—*The Hound of the Baskervilles*

PRESS, USES OF THE

"The Press, Watson, is a most valuable institution, if you only know how to use it."

—*The Adventure of the Six Napoleons*

RIGHT, BEING IN THE

"Thrice is he armed who hath his quarrel just."

—*The Disappearance of Lady Frances Carfax*

On Self-Esteem

"I cannot agree with those who rank modesty among the virtues. To the logician all things should be seen exactly as they are, and to underestimate one's self is as much a departure from truth as to exaggerate one's own powers."

—*The Greek Interpreter*

Short Cuts, Uses of

"I take a short cut when I can get it."

—*The Adventure of the Golden Pince-Nez*

Simple Problems

"Every problem becomes very childish when once it is explained to you."

—*The Adventure of the Dancing Men*

Sleep, Lack of

"I can see that you have not slept for a night or two. That tries a man's nerves more than work, and more even than pleasure."

—*The Yellow Face*

Taking Care in the Lab

"I have to be careful for I dabble with poisons a good deal."

—A Study in Scarlet

Trifles

"It is, of course, a trifle, but there is nothing so important as trifles."

—The Man with the Twisted Lip

Trust Me

"Let the whole incident be a sealed book, and do not allow it to affect your life."

—A Case of Identity

Truth, Any

"Any truth is better than indefinite doubt."

—The Yellow Face

The Value of Humility

"That was like following the brook to the parent lake. He makes one curious but profound remark. It is that the chief proof of man's real greatness lies in his perception of his own smallness. It argues, you see, a power of comparison and of appreciation which is in itself a proof of nobility. There is much food for thought in Richter. You have not a pistol, have you?"

—The Sign of Four

WATERLOO

"We have not yet met our Waterloo, but this is our Marengo, for it begins in defeat and ends in victory."

—The Adventure of the Abbey Grange

WHEN

"We must strike while the iron is hot."

—The Adventure of the Cardboard Box

WORKING OUT

"There can be no question of the value of exercise before breakfast."

—The Adventure of Black Peter

Working the Averages
"We cannot expect to score every time."

—The Naval Treaty

Worth of Work
"Work is the best antidote to sorrow, and I have a piece of work for us both to-night which, if we can bring it to a successful conclusion, will in itself justify a man's life on this planet."

—The Adventure of the Empty House

You Could Look It Up
"Read it up—you really should. There is nothing new under the sun. It has all been done before."

—A Study in Scarlet

❧

Sciences, Forensic and Otherwise

BLOOD TEST

"Let us have some fresh blood. Now, I add this small quantity of blood to a liter of water. You perceive that the resulting mixture has the appearance of pure water. The proportion of blood cannot be more than one in a million. I have no doubt, however, that we shall be able to obtain the characteristic reaction."

—*A Study in Scarlet*

CLEVER IDEAS FROM THE EAST

"The idea of using a form of poison which could not possibly be discovered by any chemical test was just such a one as would occur to a clever and ruthless man who had had an Eastern training. The rapidity with which such a poison would take effect would also, from his point of view, be an advantage. It would be a sharp-eyed coroner, indeed, who could distinguish the two little dark punctures which would show where the poison fangs had done their work."

—The Adventure of the Speckled Band

THE LOOK OF DEATH

"Men who die from heart disease, or any sudden natural cause, never by any chance exhibit agitation upon their features."

—A Study in Scarlet

DARWIN AND MUSIC

"Do you remember what Darwin says about music? He claims that the power of producing and appreciating it existed among the human race long before the power of speech was arrived at. Perhaps that is why we are so subtly influenced by it. There are vague memories in our souls of those misty centuries when the world was in its childhood."

—A Study in Scarlet

THE EAR IN DETAIL

"There is no part of the body which varies so much as the human ear.

Each ear is as a rule quite distinctive and differs from all other ones. In last year's *Anthropological Journal* you will find two short monographs from my pen upon the subject. I had, therefore, examined the ears in the box with the eyes of an expert and had carefully noted their anatomical peculiarities. Imagine my surprise, then, when on looking at Miss Cushing I perceived that her ear corresponded exactly with the female ear which I had just inspected. The matter was entirely beyond coincidence. There was the same shortening of the pinna, the same broad curve of the upper lobe, the same convolution of the inner cartilage. In all essentials it was the same ear."

—The Adventure of the Cardboard Box

HEMOGLOBIN OR BUST

"I've found it. I've found it. I have found a re-agent which is precipitated by hemoglobin, and by nothing else."

—A Study in Scarlet

LITMUS TEST

"If this paper remains blue, all is well. If it turns red, it means a man's life."

—The Naval Treaty

PHRENOLOGY

"I presume, sir, that it is not merely for the purpose of examining my skull that you have done me the honor to call here last night and again to-day?"

—*The Hound of the Baskervilles*

TYPEWRITERS

"It is a curious thing that a typewriter has really quite as much individuality as a man's handwriting. Unless they are quite new, no two of them write exactly alike. Some letters get more worn than others, and some wear only on one side."

—*A Case of Identity*

Strategy, Tactics and Tools

ON BEING METHODICAL

"We hold several threads in our hands, and the odds are that one or other of them guides us to the truth. We may waste time in following the wrong one, but sooner or later we must come upon the right."

—*The Hound of the Baskervilles*

DETAILS

"A certain selection and discretion must be used in producing a realistic effect. This is wanting in the police report, where more stress is laid, perhaps, upon the platitudes of the magistrate than upon the details, which to an observer contain the vital essence of the whole matter. Depend upon it, there is nothing so unnatural as the commonplace."

—*A Case of Identity*

ON THE DODGE

"Well, then we must make a cross-country journey to Newhaven, and so over to Dieppe. Moriarty will again do what I should do. He will get on to Paris, mark down our luggage, and wait for two days at the depot. In the meantime we shall treat ourselves to a couple of carpet-bags, encourage the manufactures of the countries through which we travel, and make our way at our leisure into Switzerland, via Luxembourg and Basle."

—The Final Problem

THOREAU'S FISH

"Circumstantial evidence is occasionally very convincing, as when you find a trout in the milk, to quote Thoreau's example."

—The Adventure of the Noble Bachelor

THE RIGHT THREAD

"There is a thread here which we have not yet grasped and which might lead us through the tangle."

—The Adventure of the Devil's Foot

His M's

"My collection of M's is a fine one. Moriarty himself is enough to make any letter illustrious, and here is Morgan the poisoner, and Merridew of abominable memory, and Matthews, who knocked out my left canine in the waiting room at Charing Cross, and, finally, here is our friend of to-night: *Moran, Sebastian, Colonel. Unemployed. Formerly 1st Bangalore Pioneers. Born London, 1840. Son of Sir Augustus Moran, C.B., once British Minister to Persia. Educated Eton and Oxford. Served in Jowaki Campaign, Afghan Campaign, Charasiab (despatches), Sherpur, and Cabul. Author of* Heavy Game of the Western Himalayas *(1881);* Three Months in the Jungle *(1884). Address: Conduit Street. Clubs: The Anglo-Indian, the Tankerville, the Bagatelle Card Club. The second most dangerous man in London.*"

—*The Adventure of the Empty House*

Holding Back

"I have no desire to make mysteries, but it is impossible at the moment of action to enter into long and complex explanations."

—*The Adventure of the Dancing Men*

Informants, Value of

"Exactly, my dear Watson! Hence the extreme importance of Porlock. Led on by some rudimentary aspirations towards right, and encouraged by the judicious stimulation of an occasional ten-pound note sent to him by devious methods, he has once or twice given me advance information which has been of value—that highest value which anticipates and prevents rather than avenges crime."

—The Valley of Fear

One of 50 Ways to Leave London

"You will dispatch whatever luggage you intend to take by a trusty messenger unaddressed to Victoria to-night. In the morning you will send for a hansom, desiring your man to take neither the first nor the second which may present itself. Into this hansom you will jump, and you will drive to the Strand end of the Lowther Arcade, handing the address to the cabman upon a slip of paper, with a request that he will not throw it away. Have your fare ready, and the instant that your cab stops, dash through the Arcade, timing yourself to reach the other side at a quarter-past nine. You will find a small brougham waiting close to the curb, driven by a fellow with a heavy black cloak tipped at the collar with red. Into this you will step, and you will reach Victoria in time for the Continental express."

—The Final Problem

A Less-Than-Subtle Method

"Well, there's nothing for it now but a direct frontal assault. Are you armed?"

—The Disappearance of Lady Frances Carfax

Malingering, Techniques of

"Three days of absolute fast does not improve one's beauty, Watson. For the rest, there is nothing which a sponge may not cure. With vaseline upon one's forehead, belladonna in one's eyes, rouge over the cheek-bones, and crusts of beeswax round one's lips, a very satisfying effect can be produced. Malingering is a subject upon which I have sometimes thought of writing a monograph. A little occasional talk about half-crowns, oysters, or any other extraneous subject produces a pleasing effect of delirium."

—The Adventure of the Dying Detective

Old Hounds on the Scent

"In the meantime I will do a little quiet work at your own doors, and perhaps the scent is not so cold but that two old hounds like Watson and myself may get a sniff of it."

—*The Adventure of the Priory School*

Problem with Pencils and Pens

"It is a pity he did not write in pencil. As you have no doubt frequently observed, the impression usually goes through—a fact which has dissolved many a happy marriage. However, I can find no trace here. I rejoice, however, to perceive that he wrote with a broad-pointed quill pen, and I can hardly doubt that we will find some impression upon this blotting-pad. Ah, yes, surely this is the very thing!"

—*The Adventure of the Missing Three-Quarter*

Always Pack the Proper Means of Persuasion

"I should be very much obliged if you would slip your revolver into your pocket. An Eley's No. 2 is an excellent argument with gentlemen who can twist steel pokers into knots. That and a tooth-brush are, I think, all that we need."

—*The Adventure of the Speckled Band*

REVENGE

"I think there are certain crimes which the law cannot touch, and which therefore, to some extent, justify private revenge."

—*The Adventure of Charles Augustus Milverton*

THE RIGHT TOOL

"Here is my lens. You know my methods."

—*The Adventure of the Blue Carbuncle*

CHECKING THE SCENE

"There is nothing like first-hand evidence, as a matter of fact, my mind is entirely made up upon the case, but still we may as well learn all that is to be learned."

—*A Study in Scarlet*

Tires

"I am familiar with forty-two different impressions left by tires."

—*The Adventure of the Priory School*

Youth, Uses of

"The mere sight of an official-looking person seals men's lips. These youngsters, however, go everywhere and hear everything. They are as sharp as needles, too; all they want is organization."

—*A Study in Scarlet*

Setting the Scene

"Surely our profession, Mr. Mac, would be a drab and sordid one if we did not sometimes set the scene so as to glorify our results. The blunt accusation, the brutal tap upon the shoulder—what can one make of such a denouement? But the quick inference, the subtle trap, the clever forecast of coming events, the triumphant vindication of bold theories—are these not the pride and the justification of our life's work?"

—*The Valley of Fear*

ON HANDWRITING

"You may not be aware that the deduction of a man's age from his writing is one which has been brought to considerable accuracy by experts. In normal cases one can place a man in his true decade with tolerable confidence."

—The Reigate Puzzle

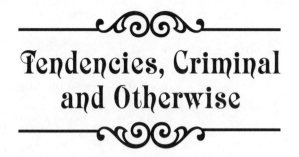

Tendencies, Criminal and Otherwise

ADVERSARIES

"He is one of my natural enemies, or, shall I say, my natural prey."
—*The Man with the Twisted Lip*

ASSASSINS

"Political assassins are only too glad to do their work and to fly."
—*A Study in Scarlet*

BLACKMAIL

"There's blackmail in it, or I am much mistaken."
—*The Yellow Face*

BROTHERLY LOVE, EXTREME

"Human nature is a strange mixture, Watson. You see that even a villain and murderer can inspire such affection that his brother turns to suicide when he learns that his neck is forfeited."

—*The Stock-Broker's Clerk*

BURGLARS' LEISURE

"As a matter of fact, burglars who have done a good stroke of business are, as a rule, only too glad to enjoy the proceeds in peace and quiet without embarking on another perilous undertaking."

—*The Adventure of the Abbey Grange*

BURGLARS' METHODS

"It is unusual for burglars to operate at so early an hour, it is unusual for burglars to strike a lady to prevent her screaming, since one would imagine that was the sure way to make her scream, it is unusual for them to commit murder when their numbers are sufficient to overpower one man, it is unusual for them to be content with a limited plunder when there was much more within their reach, and finally, I should say, that it was very unusual for such men to leave a bottle half empty."

—*The Adventure of the Abbey Grange*

A Career Criminal, Prognosis for

"That fellow will rise from crime to crime until he does something very bad, and ends on a gallows."

—*A Case of Identity*

The Commonplace Crime

"It is a mistake to confound strangeness with mystery. The most commonplace crime is often the most mysterious, because it presents no new or special features from which deductions may be drawn."

—*A Study in Scarlet*

Convenient Criminals

"If criminals would always schedule their movements like railway trains, it would certainly be more convenient for all of us."

—*The Valley of Fear*

Criminals and the Grotesque

"If you cast your mind back to some of those narratives with which you have afflicted a long-suffering public, you will recognize how often the grotesque has deepened into the criminal. Think of that little affair of the red-headed men. That was grotesque enough in the outset and yet it ended in a desperate attempt at robbery. Or, again, there was that most grotesque affair of the five orange pips, which led to a murderous conspiracy. The word puts me on the alert."

—The Adventure of Wisteria Lodge

CRIMINALS ON THE CLOCK

"They will not lose a minute, for the sooner they do their work the longer time they will have for their escape."

—The Red-Headed League

DISCIPLINE OF CRIMINALS

"In the first place, I may tell you that Moriarty rules with a rod of iron over his people. His discipline is tremendous. There is only one punishment in his code. It is death."

—The Valley of Fear

ON DOCTORS OF DEATH

"Subtle enough and horrible enough. When a doctor does go wrong he is the first of criminals. He has nerve and he has knowledge."

—The Adventure of the Speckled Band

HARD CASES

"The most difficult crime to track is the one which is purposeless."

—*The Naval Treaty*

THE HIDDEN HAND

"There is no one who knows the higher criminal world of London so well as I do. For years past I have continually been conscious of some power behind the malefactor, some deep organizing power which forever stands in the way of the law, and throws its shield over the wrong-doer. Again and again in cases of the most varying sorts—forgery cases, robberies, murders—I have felt the presence of this force, and I have deduced its action in many of those undiscovered crimes in which I have not been personally consulted. For years I have endeavored to break through the veil which shrouded it, and at last the time came when I seized my thread and followed it, until it led me, after a thousand cunning windings, to ex-Professor Moriarty, of mathematical celebrity."

—*The Final Problem*

A HIT, A PALPABLE HIT

"Plumb in the middle of the back of the head and smack through the brain. He was the best shot in India, and I expect that there are few better in London. Have you heard the name?"

—The Adventure of the Empty House

THE KILLER

"There has been murder done, and the murderer was a man. He was more than six feet high, was in the prime of life, had small feet for his height, wore coarse, square-toed boots and smoked a Trichinopoly cigar. He came here with his victim in a four-wheeled cab, which was drawn by a horse with three old shoes and one new one on his off fore-leg. In all probability the murderer had a florid face, and the finger-nails of his right hand were remarkably long. These are only a few indications, but they may assist you."

—A Study in Scarlet

MASTER CRIMINALS, TECHNIQUES OF

"There is a master hand here. It is no case of sawed-off shotguns and clumsy six-shooters. You can tell an old master by the sweep of his brush. I can tell a Moriarty when I see one. This crime is from London, not from America."

—The Valley of Fear

THE MILVERTON METHOD

"He is the king of all the blackmailers. Heaven help the man, and still more the woman, whose secret and reputation come into the power of Milverton! With a smiling face and a heart of marble, he will squeeze and squeeze until he has drained them dry. The fellow is a genius in his way, and would have made his mark in some more savoury trade. His method is as follows: He allows it to be known that he is prepared to pay very high sums for letters which compromise people of wealth and position. He receives these wares not only from treacherous valets or maids, but frequently from genteel ruffians, who have gained the confidence and affection of trusting women. He deals with no niggard hand. I happen to know that he paid seven hundred pounds to a footman for a note two lines in length, and that the ruin of a noble family was the result. Everything which is in the market goes to Milverton, and there are hundreds in this great city who turn white at his name. No one knows where his grip may fall, for he is far too rich and far too cunning to work from hand to mouth. He will hold a card back for years in order to play it at the moment when the stake is best worth winning. I have said that he is the worst man in London, and I would ask you how could one compare the ruffian, who in hot blood bludgeons his mate, with this man, who methodically and at his leisure tortures the soul and wrings the nerves in order to add to his already swollen money-bags?"

—The Adventure of Charles Augustus Milverton

OLD DOG, OLD TRICKS

"The cunning dog has covered his tracks. He has left nothing to incriminate him."

—The Adventure of the Bruce-Partington Plans

THE REPTILE OF CRIME

"Do you feel a creeping, shrinking sensation, Watson, when you stand before the serpents in the Zoo, and see the slithery, gliding, venomous creatures, with their deadly eyes and wicked, flattened faces? Well, that's how Milverton impresses me. I've had to do with fifty murderers in my career, but the worst of them never gave me the repulsion which I have for this fellow. And yet I can't get out of doing business with him—indeed, he is here at my invitation."

—The Adventure of Charles Augustus Milverton

SIMPLE CRIMES

"The larger crimes are apt to be the simpler, for the bigger the crime the more obvious, as a rule, is the motive."

—A Case of Identity

SLOW CRIMINALS
"The London criminal is certainly a dull fellow."
—*The Adventure of the Bruce-Partington Plans*

SMART CRIMINALS
"Like most clever criminals, he may be too confident in his own cleverness and imagine that he has completely deceived us."
—*The Hound of the Baskervilles*

STRANGE SYMPATHIES
"My sympathies are with the criminals rather than with the victim."
—*The Adventure of Charles Augustus Milverton*

SPIDER
"He sits motionless, like a spider in the center of its web, but that web has a thousand radiations, and he knows well every quiver of each of them."
—*The Final Problem*

The Business of Business

ALIAS WHAT?

"It is always awkward doing business with an alias."

—The Adventure of the Blue Carbuncle

AMERICAN BUSINESS PRINCIPLES

"Six thousand a year. That's paying for brains, you see—the American business principle. I learned that detail quite by chance. It's more than the Prime Minister gets. That gives you an idea of Moriarty's gains and of the scale on which he works. Another point: I made it my business to hunt down some of Moriarty's checks lately—just common innocent checks that he pays his household bills with. They were drawn on six different banks. Does that make any impression on your mind?"

—The Valley of Fear

Bank Early, Bank Often

"I have a check for five hundred pounds which should be cashed early, for the drawer is quite capable of stopping it, if he can."

—*His Last Bow*

Central Skill

"It is my business to know things. Perhaps I have trained myself to see what others overlook."

—*A Case of Identity*

On Consulting

"They are mostly sent on by private inquiry agencies. They are all people who are in trouble about something and want a little enlightening. I listen to their story, they listen to my comments, and then I pocket my fee."

—*A Study of Scarlet*

Counter-Intelligence Schemes

"They will at least show our people what is known and what is not. I may say that a good many of these papers have come through me, and I need not add are thoroughly untrustworthy. It would brighten my declining years to see a German cruiser navigating the Solent according to the mine-field plans which I have furnished."

—*His Last Bow*

LESSER OF TWO EVILS

"Once or twice in my career I feel that I have done more real harm by my discovery of the criminal than ever he had done by his crime. I have learned caution now, and I had rather play tricks with the law of England than with my own conscience."

—*The Adventure of the Abbey Grange*

MAKING A LIVING ON THEORIES

"Yes; I have a turn both for observation and for deduction. The theories which I have expressed there, and which appear to you to be so chimerical, are really extremely practical—so practical that I depend upon them for my bread and cheese."

—*A Study in Scarlet*

MONEY AND WORK

"There's money in this case, Watson, if there is nothing else."

—A Scandal in Bohemia

NUT CRUSHING, EFFECTIVE

"Because it is done by a man who cannot afford to fail, one whose whole unique position depends upon the fact that all he does must succeed. A great brain and a huge organization have been turned to the extinction of one man. It is crushing the nut with the trip-hammer—an absurd extravagance of energy—but the nut is very effectually crushed all the same."

—The Valley of Fear

PLEASE CONFUSE ME WITH THE FACTS

"I am glad of all details, whether they seem to you to be relevant or not."

—The Adventure of the Copper Beeches

POINT OF VIEW

"I put myself in the man's place, and, having first gauged his intelligence, I try to imagine how I should myself have proceeded under the same circumstances."

—The Musgrave Ritual

THE CHIEF EXECUTIVE OFFICER

"He does little himself. He only plans. But his agents are numerous and splendidly organized. Is there a crime to be done, a paper to be abstracted, we will say, a house to be rifled, a man to be removed the word is passed to the professor, the matter is organized and carried out. The agent may be caught. In that case money is found for his bail or his defense. But the central power which uses the agent is never caught—never so much as suspected."

—The Final Problem

The World, Flesh and the Devil

THE BIZARRE

"As a rule, the more bizarre a thing is the less mysterious it proves to be. It is your commonplace, featureless crimes which are really puzzling, just as a commonplace face is the most difficult to identify."

—*The Red-Headed League*

COUNTRY PLEASURES

"I'm sure, Watson, a week in the country will be invaluable to you. It is very pleasant to see the first green shoots upon the hedges and the catkins on the hazels once again. With a spud, a tin box, and an elementary book on botany, there are instructive days to be spent."

—*The Adventure of Wisteria Lodge*

COUNTRY REFRESHMENTS

"Watson, I think our quiet rest in the country has been a distinct success and I shall certainly return, much invigorated, to Baker Street to-morrow."

—The Reigate Puzzle

THE COUNTRYSIDE, HORRORS OF

"They always fill me with a certain horror. It is my belief, Watson, founded upon my experience, that the lowest and vilest alleys in London do not present a more dreadful record of sin than does the smiling and beautiful countryside."

—The Adventure of the Copper Beeches

CREEPY LOCALE

"Yes, the setting is a worthy one. If the devil did desire to have a hand in the affairs of men . . ."

—The Hound of the Baskervilles

GREAT BEAST

"Pshaw, my dear fellow, what do the public, the great unobservant public, who could hardly tell a weaver by his tooth or a compositor by his left thumb, care about the finer shades of analysis and deduction!"

—The Adventure of the Copper Beeches

On Hiding Places

"Ah, Mr. Mac, you would not read that excellent local compilation which described the concealment of King Charles. People did not hide in those days without excellent hiding places, and the hiding place that has once been used may be again."

—The Valley of Fear

The Killing Fog

"Look out of this window, Watson. See how the figures loom up, are dimly seen, and then blend once more into the cloud-bank. The thief or the murderer could roam London on such a day as the tiger does the jungle, unseen until he pounces, and then evident only to his victim."

—The Adventure of the Bruce-Partington Plans

HIS LACK OF EXERCISE
"My body has remained in this armchair and has, I regret to observe, consumed in my absence two large pots of coffee and an incredible amount of tobacco."

—The Hound of the Baskervilles

LATIN WEATHER
"It is well they don't have days of fog in Latin countries—the countries of assassination."

—The Adventure of the Bruce-Partington Plans

LOCAL SATANS
"A devil with merely local powers like a parish vestry would be too inconceivable a thing."

—The Hound of the Baskervilles

LONDON
"It's a hobby of mine to have an exact knowledge of London."

—The Red-Headed League

THE LONDON EFFECT

"No, no. No crime. Only one of those whimsical little incidents which will happen when you have four million human beings all jostling each other within the space of a few square miles. Amid the action and reaction of so dense a swarm of humanity, every possible combination of events may be expected to take place, and many a little problem will be presented which may be striking and bizarre without being criminal."

—The Adventure of the Blue Carbuncle

MORE THAN A CHEST COLD

"I know what is the matter with me. It is a coolie disease from Sumatra—a thing that the Dutch know more about than we, though they have made little of it up to date. One thing only is certain. It is infallibly deadly, and it is horribly contagious."

—The Adventure of the Dying Detective

MUSIC HATH CHARMS

"There is nothing more to be said or to be done to-night, so hand me over my violin and let us try to forget for half an hour the miserable weather and the still more miserable ways of our fellow-men."

—The Five Orange Pips

Music Hath More Charms

"A sandwich and a cup of coffee, and then off to violin-land, where all is sweetness and delicacy and harmony, and there are no red-headed clients to vex us with their conundrums."

—The Red-Headed League

In Need of Nature

"Let us walk in these beautiful woods and give a few hours to the birds and flowers."

—The Adventure of Black Peter

On Northern Air

"This northern air is invigorating and pleasant, so I propose to spend a few days upon your moors, and to occupy my mind as best I may."

—The Adventure of the Priory School

OLD PERSIAN SAWS

"You may remember the old Persian saying, 'There is danger for him who taketh the tiger cub, and danger also for who so snatches a delusion from a woman.' There is as much sense in Hafiz as in Horace, and as much knowledge of the world."

—*A Case of Identity*

SHARING ONE'S STASH

"It is cocaine, a seven-per-cent solution. Would you care to try it?"

—*The Sign of Four*

A SEA OF OYSTERS

"Indeed, I cannot think why the whole bed of the ocean is not one solid mass of oysters, so prolific the creatures seem. No doubt there are natural enemies which limit the increase of the creatures. Shall the world, then, be overrun by oysters? No, no; horrible!"

—*The Adventure of the Dying Detective*

THE PASTORAL, DARK SIDE OF

"The pressure of public opinion can do in the town what the law cannot accomplish. There is no lane so vile that the scream of a tortured child, or the thud of a drunkard's blow, does not beget sympathy and indignation among the neighbors, and then the whole machinery of justice is ever so close that a word of complaint can set it going, and there is but a step between the crime and the dock. But look at these lonely houses, each in its own fields, filled for the most part with poor ignorant folk who know little of the law. Think of the deeds of hellish cruelty, the hidden wickedness which may go on, year in, year out, in such places, and none the wiser."

—*The Adventure of the Copper Beeches*

Personals in Newspapers

"Dear me, what a chorus of groans, cries, and bleatings! What a ragbag of singular happenings! But surely the most valuable huntingground that ever was given to a student of the unusual!"

—*The Adventure of the Red Circle*

Places of Low Degree

"Had I been recognized in that den my life would not have been worth an hour's purchase; for I have used it before now for my own purposes, and the rascally lascar who runs it has sworn to have vengeance upon me. There is a trap-door at the back of that build-ing, near the corner of Paul's Wharf, which could tell some strange tales of what has passed through it upon the moonless nights. We should be rich men if we had £1000 for every poor devil who has been done to death in that den. It is the vilest murder-trap on the whole riverside."

—The Man with the Twisted Lip

STRANGE DAZE

"Well, Watson, we seem to have fallen upon evil days."

—The Adventure of the Dying Detective

AN UNINTERESTING CITY

"From the point of view of the criminal expert, London has become a singularly uninteresting city since the death of the late lamented Professor Moriarty."

—The Adventure of the Norwood Builder

Why There'll Always Be an England

ENGLISH LAW

"The English law is in the main a just law."

—*The Valley of Fear*

ENGLISH SCHOOLS

"The board-schools. Light-houses, my boy! Beacons of the future! Capsules with hundreds of bright little seeds in each, out of which will spring the wiser, better England of the future."

—*The Naval Treaty*

BRITISH LAW, CONSTANCY OF

"However, wretch as he was, he was still living under the shield of British law, and I have no doubt, Inspector, that you will see that, though that shield may fail to guard, the sword of justice is still there to avenge."

—The Resident Patient

A Museum Piece

"The famous air-gun of Von Herder will embellish the Scotland Yard Museum, and once again Mr. Sherlock Holmes is free to devote his life to examining those interesting little problems which the complex life of London so plentifully presents."

—The Adventure of the Empty House

Watson:
The Trusty Comrade

THE MAN FROM AFGHANISTAN
"You have been in Afghanistan, I perceive."

—A Study in Scarlet

THE CLUE OF PENCILS
"Watson, I have always done you an injustice. There are others. What could this NN be? It is at the end of a word. You are aware that Johann Faber is the most common maker's name. Is it not clear that there is just as much of the pencil left as usually follows the Johann?"

—The Adventure of the Three Students

THE EXCITEMENT OF READERS

"I must admit, Watson, that you have some power of selection, which atones for much which I deplore in your narratives. Your fatal habit of looking at everything from the point of view of a story instead of as a scientific exercise has ruined what might have been an instructive and even classical series of demonstrations. You slur over work of the utmost finesse and delicacy, in order to dwell upon sensational details which may excite, but cannot possibly instruct, the reader."

—The Adventure of the Abbey Grange

THE STANDARD HOLMES JURY

"Watson, you are a British jury, and I never met a man who was more eminently fitted to represent one."

—The Adventure of the Abbey Grange

HONEST WATSON

"Among your many talents dissimulation finds no place."

—The Adventure of the Dying Detective

LIMITS OF DR. WATSON

"Shall I demonstrate your own ignorance? What do you know, pray, of Tapanuli fever? What do you know of the black Formosa corruption? There are many problems of disease, many strange pathological possibilities, in the East. I have learned so much during some recent researches which have a medico-criminal aspect. It was in the course of them that I contracted this complaint. You can do nothing."

—The Adventure of the Dying Detective

THE LITERARY WATSON

"I suppose, Watson, we must look upon you as a man of letters. How do you define the word 'grotesque'?"

—The Adventure of Wisteria Lodge

MEETING OLD FRIENDS

"I've hardly seen you in the light yet. How have the years used you? You look the same blithe boy as ever."

—His Last Bow

BOLD STEPS, THE NEED FOR TAKING

"On the contrary, Watson, you can see everything. You fail, however, to reason from what you see. You are too timid in drawing your inferences."

—*The Adventure of the Blue Carbuncle*

ORDER OUT OF CHAOS

"A chaotic case, my dear Watson. It will not be possible for you to present it in that compact form which is dear to your heart. It covers two continents, concerns two groups of mysterious persons, and is further complicated by the highly respectable presence of our friend, Scott Eccles, whose inclusion shows me that the deceased Garcia had a scheming mind and a well-developed instinct of self-preservation. It is remarkable only for the fact that amid a perfect jungle of possibilities we, with our worthy collaborator, the inspector, have kept our close hold on the essentials and so been guided along the crooked and winding path. Is there any point which is not quite clear to you?"

—*The Adventure of Wisteria Lodge*

SIDEKICKS

"Oh, a trusty comrade is always of use; and a chronicler still more so."

—*The Man with the Twisted Lip*

Silent Partners

"You have a grand gift of silence. It makes you quite invaluable as a companion. 'Pon my word, it is a great thing for me to have someone to talk to, for my own thoughts are not over-pleasant."

—*The Man with the Twisted Lip*

Summing Up Watson

"I cannot at the moment recall any possible blunder which you have omitted. The total effect of your proceeding has been to give the alarm everywhere and yet to discover nothing."

—*The Disappearance of Lady Frances Carfax*

Watson, His Narrative Methods

"You are like my friend, Dr. Watson, who has a bad habit of telling his stories wrong and foremost. Please arrange your thoughts and let me know, in their due sequence, exactly what those events are which have sent you out unbrushed and unkempt, with dress boots and waistcoat buttoned awry, in search of advice and assistance."

—*The Adventure of Wisteria Lodge*

WATSON, HIS QUESTIONS

"There is an appalling directness about your questions, Watson. They come at me like bullets."

—The Valley of Fear

WATSON, HIS ROLE

"I am lost without my Boswell."

—A Scandal in Bohemia

WATSON, HIS SHREWDNESS

"Your native shrewdness, my dear Watson, that innate cunning which is the delight of your friends, would surely prevent you from enclosing cipher and message in the same envelope. Should it miscarry, you are undone."

—The Valley of Fear

WATSON, PURE WATSON

"A very commonplace little murder. You've got something better, I fancy. You are the stormy petrel of crime, Watson. What is it?"

—The Naval Treaty

WATSON, SENSE OF HUMOR
"A touch! A distinct touch! You are developing a certain unexpected vein of pawky humor, Watson, against which I must learn to guard myself."

—*The Valley of Fear*

WATSON, USES OF
"I am bound to say that in all the accounts which you have been so good as to give of my own small achievements you have habitually underrated your own abilities. It may be that you are not yourself luminous, but you are a conductor of light. Some people without possessing genius have a remarkable power of stimulating it. I confess, my dear fellow, that I am very much in your debt."

—*The Hound of the Baskervilles*

WATSON, GIVING PAIN TO
"I am pleased to think that I shall be able to free society from any further effects of his presence, though I fear that it is at a cost which will give pain to my friends, and especially, my dear Watson, to you."

—*The Final Problem*

WATSON'S EXPERTISE

"Now, Watson, the fair sex is your department."

—The Adventure of the Second Stain

WHAT GOES AROUND

"Very sorry to knock you up, Watson, but it's the common lot this morning. Mrs. Hudson has been knocked up, she retorted upon me, and I on you."

—The Adventure of the Speckled Band

ROOMMATE FROM HELL

"I say, Watson, would you be afraid to sleep in the same room with a lunatic, a man with softening of the brain, an idiot whose mind has lost its grip?"

—The Valley of Fear

DEGRADATION

"If I claim full justice for my art, it is because it is an impersonal thing—a thing beyond myself. Crime is common. Logic is rare.

Therefore it is upon the logic rather than upon the crime that you should dwell. You have degraded what should have been a course of lectures into a series of tales."

—*The Adventure of the Copper Beeches*

The Reasoner's Reasoning

PERFECTED REASON

"The ideal reasoner would, when he had once been shown a single fact in all its bearings, deduce from it not only all the chain of events which led up to it but also the results which would follow from it. As Cuvier could correctly describe a whole animal by the contemplation of a single bone, so the observer who has thoroughly understood one link in a series of incidents should be able to accurately state all the other ones, both before and after. We have not yet grasped the results which the reason alone can attain to. Problems may be solved in the study which have baffled all those who have sought a solution by the aid of their senses. To carry the art, however, to its highest pitch, it is necessary that the reasoner should be able to utilize all the facts which have come to his knowledge; and this in itself implies, as you will readily see, a possession of all knowledge, which, even in these days of free education and encyclopedias, is a somewhat rare accomplishment. It is not so impossible, however, that a man should possess all knowledge which is likely to be useful to him in his work, and this I have endeavored in my case to do."

—*The Five Orange Pips*

THE PERIL OF PREMATURE SPECULATION

"I have no data yet. It is a capital mistake to theorize before one has data. Insensibly one begins to twist facts to suit theories, instead of theories to suit facts."

—*A Scandal in Bohemia*

PRAGMATIC REALISM

"I take it in the first place that neither of us is prepared to admit diabolical intrusions into the affairs of men."

—*The Adventure of the Devil's Foot*

ON PRESUMPTION

"I presume nothing."

—*The Hound of the Baskervilles*

The Realms of Conjecture

"Ah!, there we come into those realms of conjecture, where the most logical mind may be at fault. Each may form his own hypothesis upon the present evidence, and yours is as likely to be correct as mine."

—The Adventure of the Empty House

Sifting the Sands of Surmise, Conjecture, and Hypothesis

"It is one of those cases where the art of the reasoner should be used rather for the sifting of details than for the acquiring of fresh evidence. The tragedy has been so uncommon, so complete, and of such personal importance to so many people that we are suffering from a plethora of surmise, conjecture, and hypothesis. The difficulty is to detach the framework of fact—of absolute undeniable fact from the embellishments of theorists and reporters. Then, having established ourselves upon this sound basis, it is our duty to see what inferences may be drawn and what are the special points upon which the whole mystery turns."

—Silver Blaze

SIZE OF THE PROBLEM

"It is quite a three-pipe problem."

—The Red-Headed League

SPECIAL POWERS

"Perhaps, when a man has special knowledge and special powers like my own, it rather encourages him to seek a complex explanation when a simpler one is at hand."

—The Adventure of the Abbey Grange

TAKING ONE'S TIME

"It is a capital mistake to theorize before you have all the evidence. It biases the judgment."

—A Study in Scarlet

TOO MANY CLUES

"The principal difficulty lay in the fact of there being too much evidence. What was vital was overlaid and hidden by what was irrelevant."

—The Naval Treaty

THE TRIVIAL

"The smallest point may be the most essential."

—*The Adventure of the Red Circle*

WHEN TO FOLD

"When I went into this case with you I bargained, as you will no doubt remember, that I should not present you with half-proved theories, but that I should retain and work out my own ideas until I had satisfied myself that they were correct. For this reason I am not at the present moment telling you all that is in my mind. On the other hand, I said that I would play the game fairly by you, and I do not think it is a fair game to allow you for one unnecessary moment to waste your energies upon a profitless task. Therefore I am here to advise you this morning, and my advice to you is summed up in three words—abandon the case."

—*The Valley of Fear*

WORKING BACKWARD

"The case is one where, as in the investigations which you have chronicled under the names of 'A Study in Scarlet' and of 'The Sign of Four,' we have been compelled to reason backward from effects to causes."

—*The Adventure of the Cardboard Box*

MARRIAGE, REASONS FOR ENGAGING IN

"But love is an emotional thing, and whatever is emotional is opposed to that true cold reason which I place above all things. I should never marry myself, lest I bias my judgment."

—*The Sign of Four*

INTERSECTIONS

"Now we will take another line of reasoning. When you follow two separate chains of thought, you will find some point of intersection which should approximate to the truth."

—*The Disappearance of Lady Frances Carfax*

ON THE NEED TO RE-STATE

"It is impossible as I state it, and therefore I must in some respect have stated it wrong."

—*The Adventure of the Priory School*

THE UNLIKELY EXPLANATION

"Improbable as it is, all other explanations are more improbable still."

—Silver Blaze

STRIKING A BALANCE

"We balance probabilities and choose the most likely. It is the scientific use of the imagination."

—The Hound of the Baskervilles

Memories, Schemes and Reflections

Pride, Injured
"That hurts my pride, Watson. It is a petty feeling, no doubt, but it hurts my pride."

—The Five Orange Pips

A Profession, Not a Hobby
"And that recommendation, with the exaggerated estimate of my ability with which he prefaced it, was, if you will believe me, Watson, the very first thing which ever made me feel that a profession might be made out of what had up to that time been the merest hobby."

—The "Gloria Scott"

Quiet Talk, the Last
"Stand with me here upon the terrace, for it may be the last quiet talk that we shall ever have."

—His Last Bow

Results, the Best

"Results without causes are much more impressive."

—*The Adventure of the Speckled Band*

Reputation

"I begin to think that I make a mistake in explaining. Omne ignotum pro magnifico, you know, and my poor little reputation, such as it is, will suffer shipwreck if I am so candid."

—*The Red-Headed League*

The Strangest Case

"The Cornish horror—strangest case I have handled."

—*The Adventure of the Devil's Foot*

Technical Writer and Tobacco

"Yes, I have been guilty of several monographs. They are all upon technical subjects. Here, for example, is one 'Upon the Distinction between the Ashes of the Various Tobaccos.' In it I enumerate a hundred and forty forms of cigar, cigarette, and pipe tobacco, with colored plates illustrating the difference in the ash. It is a point which is continually turning up in criminal trials, and which is sometimes of supreme importance as a clue. If you can say definitely, for example, that some murder had been done by a man who was smoking an Indian lunkah, it obviously narrows your field of search. To the trained eye there is as much difference between the black ash of a Trichinopoly and the white fluff of bird's-eye as there is between a cabbage and a potato."

—The Sign of Four

THE BLOODHOUND'S NOSE

"A draghound will follow aniseed from here to John O'Groat's, and our friend, Armstrong, would have to drive through the Cam before he would shake Pompey off his trail."

—The Adventure of the Missing Three-Quarter

ON HERD ANIMALS

"The horse is a very gregarious creature."

—Silver Blaze

The Game's Forever Afoot!

PLAYING THE PERCENTAGES

"Winwood Reade is good upon the subject. He remarks that, while the individual man is an insoluble puzzle, in the aggregate he becomes a mathematical certainty. You can, for example, never foretell what any one man will do, but you can say with precision what an average number will be up to. Individuals vary, but percentages remain constant. So says the statistician."

—*The Sign of Four*

PLAYING YOUR HAND

"The shadow has departed and will not return. We must see what further cards we have in our hands and play them with decision. Could you swear to that man's face within the cab?"

—*The Hound of the Baskervilles*

Strike Up the Band

"The band! The speckled band!"

—*The Adventure of the Speckled Band*

Victorian Rock Climbing

"I stood up and examined the rocky wall behind me. In your picturesque account of the matter, which I read with great interest some months later, you assert that the wall was sheer. That was not literally true. A few small footholds presented themselves, and there was some indication of a ledge. The cliff is so high that to climb it all was an obvious impossibility, and it was equally impossible to make my way along the wet path without leaving some tracks. I might, it is true, have reversed my boots, as I have done on similar occasions, but the sight of three sets of tracks in one direction would certainly have suggested a deception. On the whole, then, it was best that I should risk the climb. It was not a pleasant business. The fall roared beneath me. I am not a fanciful person, but I give you my word that I seemed to hear Moriarty's voice screaming at me out of the abyss. A mistake would have been fatal. More than once, as tufts of grass came out in my hand or my foot slipped in the wet notches of the rock, I thought that I was gone. But I struggled upward, and at last I reached a ledge several feet deep and covered with soft green moss, where I could lie unseen, in the most perfect comfort. There I was stretched, when you, my dear Watson, and all your following were investigating in the most sympathetic and inefficient manner the circumstances of my death."

—The Adventure of the Empty House

RUDE AWAKENINGS

"Come, Watson, come! The game is afoot. Not a word! Into your clothes and come!"

—The Adventure of the Abbey Grange

❦